beheading the virgin mary
and other stories

DONAL McLAUGHLIN

beheading

the

virgin

mary,

and

other

stories

DALKEY ARCHIVE PRESS
Champaign / London / Dublin

Library of Congress Cataloging-in-Publication Data
McLaughlin, Donal, 1961-
    Beheading the Virgin Mary & other stories / Donal McLaughlin. – First edition.
    pages cm
    ISBN 978-1-62897-012-8 (pbk. : alk. paper)
    1. Scotland--Social life and customs – Fiction.
    2. Northern Ireland--Social life and customs – Fiction.
    I. Title.
    PR6113.C525B55 2014
    823'.92--dc23
                    2014001104

This publication was partially supported by the Illinois Arts Council, a state agency,
and the University of Illinois (Urbana-Champaign).

beheading the virgin mary received financial assistance
from the Arts Council of Ireland.

www.dalkeyarchive.com

Cover: design and composition by Mikhail Iliatov
Printed on permanent/durable and acid-free paperv

contents

bonus material

stella
in memoriam

big trouble
October 1968

Liam knew when he woke that morning something was going to happen.

It was a year, maybe, since they'd left Derry to go & live in the country. An' one of them bright sunny mornings when his mammy & daddy took *forever* to get up. An' something was *definitely* telling him something was going to happen.

He rose, anyhow. All Sean done, when he did, was roll over. Cahal, likewise, was completely out for the count. His sisters but were up—he could hear them. Annette & Ciara, anyway. Up to something, they were, he reckoned. Liam might've been seven & might've been the eldest. Them two were thick as thieves but.

He went for a wee-wee first, then headed into the scullery. The girls had been up for donkeys, looked like. Finished their cornflakes, they were, & doing the dishes already. It was good they were trying to help. Liam, himself, was too. It wasn't long since God had taken their gran, sure, & Daddy'd asked the big ones to *try 'n' help*. They could be getting a new wee baby was the other thing he'd said. Mammy'd need help on that front too. Three each, it was at the minute—so Liam was hoping, this time, the boys would go into the lead.

'You don't take cornflakes, don't you not, Liam?' Annette checked.

He shook his head just & she put them back in the larder. He took a taste of crispies instead & Ciara passed him the milk. He poured some, listened for the snack-crackle-pop, then started wolfing them down.

'Take your time, weeboy!' Ciara said—sactly the way their mammy would.

Whatever the girls were up to, they still weren't letting on. Liam was damned if he was going to ask. Not that *they* were shy about pestering *him*: 'We still playing the Band Song, Liam?' Ciara was soon asking.

'At some point, aye,' he answered, sounding as bad as their daddy nearly.

'Ye promised, mind!' Annette warned. 'An' the wee ones can't wait!'

He made sure it wasn't showing. Liam but, if he got his way, was for buggering off without them. He wanted *peace*. That was the advantage of the countryside. All spring & summer, he'd been watching things grow. The ladybirds & caterpillars. Catkins & pussy-willow. Even the wee black chicks till the dog next door got them.

Autumn mist, the forecast was & he was dying to see the colours: all the different colours in the trees. Autumn was on its way alright. Ye could feel the change in the air. Sun or no sun (to quote his mammy), ye could feel it.

He finished his crispies, rinsed out the plate, headed into the living-room to see what themmins were up to. Sean was finally up. Bernadette & Cahal were up & dressed now too. 'Did yis say your prayers?' Annette was asking. It was their breakfasts she should've been getting.

Liam soon seen what her & Ciara were up to. They were making firelighters. The *Journal's* big double-pages were a handful, so it was just Ciara & Annette, not the wee ones. Liam watched them starting at a corner and rolling the paper, lik their mammy always done. The bit in your hand was wee to start with, soon got longer & longer but. In no time at all, you'd a *stick*. The girls knew to wrap it round your fingers, then slip your fingers out of the ring & poke the last bit up through the middle, making sure it held. That way, you'd the wee boats their mammy put the coals on. Sure enough: soon they'd a whole collection stacked in front of the fireplace, waiting for their mammy to light them.

The weans were twiddling their thumbs now; at a loss for what to do wi themselves. Were they *blind*? Place was lik a bloody pigsty! It wasn't just the nightdresses they'd taken off to put on them. Their daddy's tie was over the settee, his shirt had fallen to the floor. His trousers were in a heap, beneath the Sacred Heart. His socks, at least, were tucked into his brogues, his cuff links & tiepin beside his Gallagher's Blues.

It wasn't like their mammy to be untidy. Her shoes were where she'd left them too but, her jacket over the door. Visitors—they must've had visitors. Empty & half-empty mugs & cups were everywhere ye looked. Plates full of crumbs were as well. A dirty spoon in the bowl had soiled the sugar.

'We definitely playing the Band Song, Liam?' a certain wee pest asked.

'Aye, Sean!' he snapped. 'Didn't I promise?'

'Not till Mammy and Daddy are up but,' he added. 'We're not allowed out till they are.'

The weans looked disappointed. Would just have to be patient.

'I know what!' he said, trying to sound excited. 'We can redd up! See who the best tidier-upper is.'

Was either that, or teach them all to spell *Czechoslovakia*.

There was a dishcloth over the back of the settee, a towel to go back to the toilet.

Liam lifted them, folded them. Headed first into the toilet, then the scullery.

'Gi'e us a hand wi these cups, Ciara, will ye?'

Ciara gathered the spoons while she was at it. Sean, seeing her, said *he*'d get the biscuits. Gave him the chance to sneak one.

The place was looking better already: Annette was busy folding Daddy's clothes, Ciara was shoving the papers under the cushions, and Bernie took the nightdresses into the bedroom. They sat down to admire the place. Aye, their mammy would be pleased. Definitely.

The one last thing was the ashtrays. Diabolical the smell was, off them. Holding their noses, Liam lifted one & Ciara the other & they marched them out to the bin.

Annette grabbed her chance. Liam was hardly back before she started her playacting.

'God, I could kill a cigarette, Liam!' she said.

The wee ones laughed.

Liam was fit for her. 'Aye, well ye can smoke your own, woman!'

He'd to laugh, himself. Specially when he spotted Cahal looking to see was it okay to laugh?

Annette pretended to huff. 'Okay, ya lousy shite—I will!' An' with a 'See if I care!' sort-of shrug & an 'I'll remember that!' kind of glare, she was down off the settee & across to the fireplace to lift the nearest "boat." The thing unfurled soon as she touched it. Not that it mattered—was the paper stick she was after, sure.

She held it to her lips, lik she was smoking. The weans laughed again. Sean jumped down to join her.

'Gi'e us one, too, Annette! Gaun!'

'Roll your own, ya big lump!' she just said.

The others were killing themselves. Sean tried, struggled wi the big sheet of paper but. Eventually, when he held his *fag* up (as he called it), it was two feet long nearly. Cahal was in kinks, so he was.

By this time, Annette had found the matches. She posed, holding the box, her bare legs wrapped round each other like Auntie Bernie's.

Ciara egged her on. 'Gaun, Annette! Light it!'

'She's goney!' Sean squealed.

She will 'n' all! Liam realised.

He thought about trying to stop her, lik his mother & father would expect him to. There was no way she'd burn herself but, he reckoned. Naw, it would fizzle out just before it got to her mouth, probably.

Annette took a match out.

'Gi'e us a light too, love, will ye?' Sean said.

He moved his head closer.

She struck the match & lit the fag & Sean, absolutely shitting himself, jumped back. The amount of smoke & speed & size of the flame were terrible. Wild flimsy the "cigarette" looked, way the flames were racing up it. Annette froze just.

'Into the grate!' Liam managed to say. 'Put it in the grate, would ye?'

She did. They watched the paper burn, the flames licking round it till they just went out by themselves.

Ye could hear the relief.

Ciara went over to Annette. 'Are ye alright?'

Sean just laughed. 'Course she is!'

Annette said she was. Ye could see she was shaking but.

'None of this would've happened if ye'd let us play the Band Song!' she tried to protest.

Liam ignored her. 'No one's to say a word about this, right? We'll be in *big* big trouble if yis do!'

'Promise me!' he insisted, lifting the charred papers—to hide them.

They promised.

Liam could just hear his daddy but, if anyone opened their mouth. He'd read the bloody Riot Act, he would. To him, especially: 'You that's made your First Holy Communion 'n' all! What age are ye now? Seven-'n'-a-half? Well, ye want to bloody act it!'

It was a good while before first their mammy & then their daddy rose & had their breakfasts.

The weans sat watching them, willing them on.

'What is it?' their da—nervous, sort of—asked.

'Nothing!' they claimed.

Their da had hardly finished before he was scooting up to his mother's. On his way home, he'd be dropping in on the Housing Association, he told their mammy. An' on the Civil Rights people.

Soon as the car drove off, their mammy got stuck in. It was high time she done the beds, she said. She thanked them for the nice 'n' tidy living room. No one mentioned the fire, thank God.

Sean waited a minute. 'Is it alright if we play out the front, Mammy?' he then called from the hall.

'Long as you're careful, aye—'

'We can do it now!' Sean raced in to tell them. 'We can play the Band Song!'

'We know! We heard!'

Ye could see he couldn't wait, Sean. The weeboy'd not shut up about it, sure, since Liam'd first told them about down the town last week. Everyone'd been talking about the big Civil Rights march. Him & his granda, but, had only seen the Orange one. Heading down the Strand, they'd been, when they stopped to watch the parade.

Liam thought the band was great. Had never seen anything like it. He loved their bowler hats. The banners, the flutes. The enormous great drums were the icing on the cake. *Lumbago drums*, his granda called them.

The tune they played was wild catchy. So much so Liam, who was constantly humming it, had the rest of them humming it too. "The Band Song" was *their* name for it. Their daddy called it "The Sash." The words were too hard for children. Ireland wasn't just Ireland, for example, but *Erin's Isle*. And the past wasn't the past but *bygone days of yore*.

'It rhymes wi *sash my father wore*,' their da explained.

'Fact it puts the fear of God into Catholics helps 'n' all,' he'd added, wi a knowing look to their mother.

Now they'd the all-clear, the rest of the mahoods couldn't get ready quick enough. Ciara & Annette appeared wi every pot in the house. They'd the lids to use as cymbals 'n' all. 'Mammy's knitting needles'll be the drumsticks,' Annette was telling the wee ones. The ones with plastic row counters gave a wild nice sound.

Liam, it was, who minded the dishcloths. He fetched them from the hot-press & put the green one round his shoulders. Annette grabbed the other. The rest made do wi toilet paper. It was comical, right enough: the way Bernie's kept tearing & Cahal's was all twisted.

The next thing they needed was hats. The closest they had was cowboy hats. Sean looked his Big Chief headdress out, was told to put it back but. 'It'll ruin the effect, weeboy,' Annette was claiming. The fruit bowl was sent back 'n' all. It wasn't that kind of orange, Liam explained to Cahal. It was a *different* kind.

He was starting to lose his patience.

'Are yis taking this seriously or not?'

'We are! We're taking it seriously!' the weans all protested.

He was lining them up in the back hall when the needles gave Liam another idea.

'Wait here!' he said.

He found an old jotter, tore all the clean pages out, returned to the kitchen wi a pen. The others watched, fascinated. Writing down names, he was. A different page for each. PAISLEY was first. O'NEILL second. FAULKNER & HUME soon followed.

Liam paused to study what he'd done. The rest, looking too, were none the wiser. Sean was the one to ask: 'What ye doing that for, Liam?'

'Ye'll see in a minute!' he said.

Ye could see he was working it out. When he lifted the pen again, it was to add IN or OUT. PAISLEY was IN & O'NEILL OUT.

HUME had to be IN. He was a friend of their da's after all & wild civil. Their gran—their *other* gran: their *daddy's* mammy—raved about him.

FAULKNER was OUT.

He done some DOWN WITH STORMONT!s while he was at it.

'You're forgetting ONE MAN, ONE VOTE,' Ciara minded him.

He done some of them 'n' all, then pierced every single page, top

& bottom. All he'd to do now was take each one & poke up a needle through the holes.

Pleased as Punch, he was, as he handed out his placards.

Tripping over themselves, the rest of them were, to get out now. Liam lined them up at the gate. Once they were all in position, he lifted the latch & they filed out, their placards under their arms. Soon they were marching along past the chapel, stopping only to bless themselves.

Beating their drums, they were.

Left, right. Left, right.

Banging the lids off the pots.

Humming for all they were worth.

Sure I am an Ulster Orangeman, Liam started giving it. *From Erin's Isle I came—*

That was all he minded but. All any of them minded. After that, it was *dih dih dih.*

They were reaching the chorus as they approached the local MACE. Mrs. Jackson was greeted wi *It is green but it is beautiful*, if ye don't mind, as she left wi her groceries. For once in her life, she smiled. She even looked as if she forgave them for the time they broke her window.

Dih dih dih dih dih-dih dih-dih-dih, dih-dih-DIH-dih dih dih dih—

It wasn't like him either: your man from above the bar smiled 'n' all but.

Me-e father wore it as a YOUTH i-in by-gone day-s of yore, Liam roared finally, his eyebrow giving the signal for the rest to join in:

And it's on the TWELFTH,
I-I love to wear—
the-e SASH me fa-a-ther wore!

Another verse & chorus & they were back at the house. Wee Cahal was full of it. 'The Band Song's great, Liam, isn't it, Liam?' he kept repeating. Right 'n' all, he was.

A pause, kind of, followed—as if they were taking a rest. Liam knew fine but what was next. Something had distracted him just. Out of the corner of his eye, he'd spotted Mrs. McKinney up at her window—her hair all over the place as usual. The oul bitch was hanging out even, big lump of a woman though she was. She looked lik she was raging—not that Liam let that stop him.

'PAISLEY IN' he chanted, punching the air with his placard. 'FAULK-NER OUT!'

The wee ones repeated it after him, waving their own placards.

It was *The News* they were playing at now, not what he seen wi his granda. The news was boring, usually. It could be scary 'n' all but—if Czechoslovakia or Paris was on. Derry wasn't scary, apart from last week. Derry being shown was normally great. His da, sure, would recognise people. An' his mammy could always spot the different places. Naw, there was no need to be feart. Not if you trusted in God, there wasn't, & if the B-Specials stayed put & didn't draw their truncheons. Last week was different but. Everybody said so. The RUC had *lashed out*. Had aimed for people's heads. On the TV, it was, when Liam got home wi his granda. Bloody brutes, his da had roared when they baton-charged the marchers.

'FITT IN!' Liam shouted next. Annette looked at him, puzzled. '*Gerry* Fitt!' he told her. 'Not *fit* wi one "t"!'

It was as if Fitt's name started Ciara singing: *We shall over-co-o-me—*

They knew the words to this one, alright. Their da had taught them in the car. The Band Song but, they all agreed, was catchier. Way folk sung this one made ye sad.

Not enough of them were joining in so Ciara gave *We shall not, we shall not be moved* a go. They didn't join in for that one either but. A few more chants of PAISLEY IN, FAULKNER OUT & that was it, more or less. Everything petered out. Cahal confusing his INs & OUTs was the final nail in the coffin. He'd the rest of them in fits, the weeboy. Shouting the sact opposite, he was, of what was wrote on their placards.

The weans, having had their fun, were heading back inside. Liam let on to do the same & shut the gate behind him. Soon as no one was looking but, he was off down the lane.

On his own, he wanted to be. To look at nature. To see how things were turning.

Unbeknown to the weeboy as he fingered fallen leaves, Mrs. McKinney was down at the door the minute their da got out of the car. Demanding to know what kinda father he was supposed to be, she was. What kinda way did he think he was rearing his youngsters? A bloody buckin disgrace, it was: way they were out there this morning, chanting & singing Protestant filth! On her way right now to the Chapel House, she was—to tell Fr. Shankley. That weeboy Liam was a disgrace. No fit example for his younger brothers & sisters. Shocking, it was. If it was a child of hers, she'd march him straight up the road to confession. Take him by the bloody ear, she would.

a recent death

His da was no sooner dead than Sean Feeney took it into his head he should speak to Kenny Carson.

It was Mr. Carson—the old principal—he'd really have needed. Matt was a long time dead but. His wife, Josie, was too.

Their son, Sean hoped, could be the answer.

One night in June already, he headed up to Beechmount. Expecting to foot it, he'd been. An uncle gave him his car but.

'Take it, youngfella!' Colum had insisted. 'Come Thursday, you'll be back in Glasgow, sure, and this is your one free evening!'

It was weird driving a route he'd only ever walked: up past the Cathedral, along the Lone Moor. The graffiti he seen told a story.

SO YOU THINK IT'S ALL OVER, ENGLAND?

His gran had had a point. Peace could come free wi your cornflakes, and there'd still be ones in Ireland who'd huff and puff.

Sean found what he thought was the house and parked up. He sat for a moment surveying the street, the wipers restoring his outlook when mizzle threatened to blur it.

Unreal, it was. Ireland, this quiet.

It was the right house alright: the orangey-coloured pebbledash, the long fish-tank window.

He'd hardly pressed the bell, Sean, when a silhouette appeared. The door opened.

'How are you doing, Kenny?' he asked.

His accent didn't register. The giant of a man just looked at him.

'It's Sean,' Sean said. 'Sean Feeney. Over from Scotland!'

'Sean!' Kenny replied, shaking his hand. 'How are you? What are you doing in Derry? God, it's good to see you! Come in!'

Kenny led the way down the hall.

'I was sorry to hear about your father,' he said.

Sean nodded just.

'I heard on my own father's anniversary, as it happens—'

'Oh!' That detail caught Sean on the hop. 'How many years is that, Kenny?'

'Sixteen.'

Sean nodded again. 'That long, eh?'

They were heading for the room he expected: the setting of previous visits. Late seventies, early eighties, as a student. End of the sixties, with his da. Kenny, first a college boy, later already working, had always taken time to be civil. Had always stuck his head round the door.

'Living room okay?'

'Sure! Why?'

'Your father couldn't face it when he visited. Too many memories, he said.'

'He was here, was he? After your father died? When would that have been?'

'Ten years ago maybe. He came up to see me, one time he was over. He was as sharp as ever. A great night's craic, we had!'

'Tell me something, Kenny: did my da ever *teach* you?'

'He did, surely! He taught up the street, sure, until my father poached him. The best teacher I had, he was. Easily. He put the basics into you permanently. Must have done so for thousands of children.'

'Teachers, eh?' Sean said. 'I've just packed it in, myself.'

They sat down either side of the fireplace: fake coals that weren't switched on. Sean clocked the accoutrements, hanging on the wee brass stand.

Sean, in the past, would've been on the settee, Matt on a hard chair opposite.

'You're your father all over!' Kenny announced.

'You think so?'

'God, aye! Looks. Mannerisms. Everything!'

Sean smiled, nodded. 'You're not the first to tell me that! Though there's plenty of Mum in me too, thankfully!'

'It must have been very sudden?' Kenny probed. 'Or had your father not been well?'

'Was sudden enough,' Sean said, 'though Mum would tell you different. She sensed he wasn't himself.'

'How is your mother?'

'Great, thanks, aye. Mum's amazing.'

He filled Kenny in. The spell in hospital before Xmas that seemed to do Dad good. The transfusions that took away the greyness. The second spell, after Xmas, when he didn't come back out.

'He was losing any blood they gave him—'

Kenny, Sean could tell, knew his way round illness. Over here they all did. The Troubles had made them all experts.

'Various tests came back clear,' he continued, prepared to give a Carson some detail. 'There were others they couldn't do though. Because of his platelets. Cancer was diagnosed eventually. A fortnight later, he died. Swift as that, it was. The family took comfort from that.'

'It's sad, nevertheless.' Kenny said. 'He was some man! More of a phenomenon than a man, is what I tell people!'

'I know. I read your letter. Mum says to thank you for it.'

'It was the least I could do.'

'I was kicking myself when I saw it. Just back from another funeral, I was. I did ask were you here, but people told me you'd moved on. You might not understand this, Kenny—since we barely know each other—but something inside me's been desperate to visit you. I idolised your dad, you know. And we both know what our fathers were like. The only two men at the school. Friends, rather than colleagues. This room could tell some stories, that's for sure!'

'You can say that again!' Kenny said, laughing.

You could see in that big laugh of his how much he relished the memories.

They got on to Sean resigning. From there, to Kenny's M.E.

'Aye, workplaces have a lot to answer for!' Sean insisted. 'It's not just the buildings are sick!'

Kenny seemed reluctant to go there.

'I haven't offered you a cuppa!' he said. 'Would you like one?'

'I'd love one!'

Kenny nipped out to put it on.

Sean, from where he was sitting, was now taking the room in. Early eighties, he'd last been here. It was Matt and Josie he minded though. Not the furniture. The room had to be as Kenny inherited it. The boy had spread himself out just. Wherever you looked lay manuals, tools, components. There were papers, stacked high, in files and boxes. The one thing you didn't see was photographs. The faces in Sean's head couldn't be checked for accuracy.

The way the stuff was piled triggered a memory: Matt taking Primary 3 once, to release their normal teacher.

'Imagine this room filled with ten-pound notes, children!' he'd urged. 'Imagine them stacked up! One on top of the other! From the floor right up to the ceiling! Imagine each stack up against the next! No space at all between them! How much money would that be now, do you think?'

The answers had varied from tens, to hundreds, to thousands of thousands—with Matt chuckling, knowingly, as the kids warmed to the task.

'What *is* the answer, sir?' someone eventually asked.

'I don't know!' Matt had admitted. 'But I do know this: not even that amount could repay the love of a parent.'

The tea-making noises were becoming more promising. Kenny would soon be back. Sean took the chance to focus on what he would ask. The question about his da he hoped Kenny could answer.

He wanted, too, to talk about Matt. He might just have been six at the start—and ten the summer they'd emigrated—he'd loved Matt Carson to bits but. He'd never forgotten the lifts—him in Matt's Cortina, racing his dad's Estate. The antics, the waves of them, each time they overtook. Matt had taught him to spell. Words like *metamorphosis.*

'You can do no bloody wrong in that man's eyes!' his da would let on to complain. 'He seems to think—though I can't think why—the sun shines out of your arse!'

The tea was ready, sounded like. Any second now, Kenny'd be back.

Sean still wasn't sure what to broach next. 'Your da thought the sun shone out of my arse' wasn't exactly an option. Nor was his other abiding image of Matt: at the side of a country road, smashed by an Army jeep. Stationary, he'd been—a-r-y, not e-r-y—when the soldiers went into him.

They'd heard about it in Scotland even.

People had phoned.

Kenny returned with two mugs.

'Sorry to keep you, Sean—I was letting it draw!'

'No problem, Kenny.'

'Milk and sugar?'

'Just black, thanks.'

'Do you know what I remember, Kenny?' Sean asked, sipping his tea too soon. 'I remember our fathers singing.'

'Oh yes—they sang, alright!'

'D'ye remember their protest songs? Them writing words to existing airs?'

'I don't, no—'

'"The West's Asleep," your dad's was called. I mind him singing it—in here, in fact! The title was meant to mean something but I never knew what.'

Sean paused, remembering. 'My own da's was more in-your-face. Full of names, it was. The names of those in power. The names of Civil Righters. The tune was "Slattery's Mounted Foot," if that means anything to you. Back then, I could sing it. At the age of eight or nine, it was my party-piece!'

Kenny smiled at the thought. You could see it didn't surprise him. Sean, without warning, launched into the chorus:

Then up from the station marched each daughter and each son,
shouting out their slogans, chanting "We shall overcome."
Fitt, McCann, O'Doherty, and McAteer as well;
they marched to face the batons, and their fate to you I'll tell.

'Sorry, should've warned you, Kenny,' he said when he'd finished. 'Singing's one thing I don't take after him!'

'Don't be so hard on yourself—that was alright!'

'You don't remember your own dad's song?'

'Can't say I do—though I've heard the original.'

'The title's all I remember. Would be nice to unearth it though. See what we make of it now.'

Kenny nodded, pensively. Was time to cheer him up, Sean reckoned.

'D'you know about the time my dad shook hands with the Reverend Ian?'

Kenny's face lit up. 'What, *Paisley*? He did not, did he?'

'He did, aye! On a school trip to Belfast. Your dad wasn't on it. Was my class that went. And my da's class. 1969, it would've been. We went to the zoo. And we went to Stormont—'

'Hope you could tell the difference!' Kenny laughed.

Sean grinned. 'The joke was made at the time! But listen to this! At Stormont, my da asked the boys in charge to fetch John Hume: could he come 'n' say hello to a group of children from Derry? Turned out Johnny wasn't available—so they brought Ian Paisley out, to see if he would do. "I bet you don't have to be told who I am, boys and girls!" the man himself boomed as he crossed the foyer. I disappeared behind a pillar. Next thing I knew, my da was shaking his hand!'

Kenny was roaring with laughter. 'I don't believe it! Your father—and Big Paisley! After all he said about him in this very room too!'

They fell silent for a moment: Sean aware of what they were sharing, suddenly; Kenny remembering his master—the later family friend.

Was Sean broke the silence.

'There's something I wanted to ask you, Kenny.'

'On you go then. Fire away.'

'Do you know why my da left Derry?'

Kenny shook his head. 'Can't say I do, Sean.'

'I know what *I* heard, or think I heard, and was wondering whether you heard the same.'

'No, I'm sorry—I don't know.' Kenny paused and looked him in the eye. 'I'd tell you if I did. What was it you heard?'

It was a long story. Sean kept it short. His da had gone for another school. Everyone reckoned he'd get it. No one had a record like him. The school, in the end, went to someone else but. His da, when he heard, was livid. Headed straight down to the priest. He'd laughed in the P.P.'s face, legend had it, when the priest told him the reason.

'Hence Scotland—which had a teacher shortage.' Sean paused, trying to read Kenny's reaction still. 'It would've been Australia, only my granda was dying.'

Kenny hadn't responded to the reason the priest gave. The shaving bit. The objection to his da bloody shaving.

'Course, why my dad shaved at lunchtimes was to look the part in the afternoons too.'

Kenny now nodded. 'What you're saying figures alright—but I'm hearing it for the first time. I can't confirm it. It tallies with stories I did hear, though.'

'He didn't have much time for certain members of the clergy, your father, did he?' Kenny added, standing up. 'You've reminded me: there's a letter in the loft. I'll go and get it. Have a look at my books while I do. Local history's a great hobby of mine.'

Kenny reached for one in the alcove next to the fire. 'Do you know this, for example?'

'I do, yeah,' Sean answered, recognising the list Kenny opened at—his da's name next to 1960.

'I know the author's other work also,' Kenny continued. 'He's in Scotland too. He's not reconstructed enough for my taste though. Hasn't moved on in outlook like people here have done. You need, these days, to be able to imagine the other side's point-of-view, sure.'

Sean stood up to replace the book as Kenny went upstairs. His head was too full to be able to look at the others. He clocked the top-shelf alcohol. Couldn't actually mind whether Matt partook.

He sat down again, that rawness about him there'd been since Dad died. He'd just made a connection, he realised, he hadn't made previously. The whole hullabaloo—his da's row with the priest— had happened at the height of the marches. There they'd been, out protesting. One man, one vote. Same work, same wage etc. It wasn't anti-Catholic discrimination his da was a victim of but. It was petty staffroom politics. The parish bloody priest.

That was what had done it. What had forced his dad to leave.

Not that they weren't better off, away from it all—

His dad had gone, sure, from hoping to return to Ireland, to hoping to retire to Ireland, to wanting to be buried in Ireland, to choosing a graveyard in Scotland.

When Kenny returned, he'd a pale-blue page in his hand.

Basildon Bond. Two sides of a letter pad.

Even from a distance, the writing was unmistakable.

'I should explain,' Kenny said. 'I'd a fire last year. And the stuff in the attic suffered. That's why all this stuff's in here—'

He pointed to the files, the boxes.

Sean took the page. One side was page two of a letter. The reverse, page five.

'I can't find the rest,' Kenny added. 'I'll send you a copy when I do.'

Sean could hardly read for shaking.

It wasn't just the ink. The royal-blue fountain pen. It was also what he was reading.

'This is what I was asking you about, Kenny. My dad's explaining to your dad what happened. This was written from Scotland. Your dad was on holiday when we left!'

'What is it your father says?'

Sean could hardly read straight, his eye kept leaping ahead. He'd to force himself to concentrate. To keep going back.

Finally, he shook his head.

'It's no use,' he said. 'We'd need page one, and what follows. He's in the middle of something here. Referring to a conversation with the priest—whether the infamous one, or not, I don't know—and to conversations with your father. He'd asked your dad's advice, clearly. Refers back to that. And to what he'd reported on the phone. But since your dad knew what was said, it's not spelled out.'

'I'll have to see if I can find the rest for you,' Kenny offered.

Sean felt himself trembling. This was amazing: just weeks after the funeral, a piece of paper was taking him back to the summer the family had emigrated.

He turned the page. Continued to read. Broke out of it almost immediately.

He thrust the letter towards Kenny.

'Take it, Kenny!' he pleaded. 'I can't read it!'

'I'll burst into tears if I do.'

'Do me a favour and post us that photocopy. The family would appreciate it.'

'I will,' Kenny said. 'I promise.'

Sean considered a second stab while the page was still in his hand. Knew deep down but, he couldn't. Kenny, sensing so too, accepted it back.

What he had been reading was a thank-you. The most beautiful expression of his da's gratitude for all Matt Carson had done for him. A beautifully constructed paragraph in his father's flawless handwriting. Phrase by phrase, line by line, it had been building towards the close he hadn't been able to read. The simplicity of it, the selflessness, was too much for him.

'Know something, Kenny?'

'What?'

'I'm five years older now than my dad was then.'

Kenny nodded just.

Nothing more was said as Sean finished his tea. Putting down his cup, he made to go.

'I'm sorry, man,' he said. 'But I'm going to have to leave you. I've an uncle to collect. And am late as it is.'

They walked down the hall.

Sean shook Kenny's hand as he stepped into the night.

'Keep in touch now!' Kenny urged.

'I will,' Sean promised.

'I'll walk you to the car!' Kenny insisted.

Sean unlatched the gate. The car was in one piece still. There hadn't been a riot.

'Things are quieter these days then?' he asked as they walked to the car.

'Troubles-wise,' he added, spotting Kenny's confusion.

'Oh, there's plenty of peace, alright!' Kenny confirmed, laughing. 'It's *reconciliation* there's not enough of!'

Kenny waved as he drove off, just as Matt always done when he'd walked away in the past.

Another Derry farewell to add to the rest.

Thirty years on, they were still happening. Only difference this time being: his da was dead and buried.

Halfway down the town, the image came back to him: of Kenny and himself, in front of the fire, talking the way they had done.

Their two das would've approved, he reckoned.

the age of reason

When they first moved over to Scotland, as ye know, the O'Donnells lived at the top of the Steps. What ye might not know is: just up the street from them was a kind of junction, a triangle of grass in the middle of the road anyhow—an *awkward place* in the middle of the road if ye lived where they lived, a pain in the arse if ye'd a pram to push. Aye, that's what it will've been: if ye lived across the street, it was no bother. There, there was a footpath, all the way along there was a footpath & it reached the brow of the hill & went down the other side. If ye were where they were but & set off up the street, the footpath veered round & up to the left, taking ye away from where ye were going. Aye, that's what it will've been, that'll be why the weans, on their way to Mass, started taking the shortcut over the grass—Liam in particular, & in particular once he got to the age he could go on his own. Once he got to that age & his mammy & daddy would've given in & let him, he'd've gone to a later Mass, sure, the lazy shite, would've had a long lie & gone at night—to the Mass introduced firstday for the workers.

That said, that contradicts the next bit cos the youngfella minds clear as a bell: on the day in question he was the furthest in in the pew, the furthest in from the aisle, wi however many of the other six weans to his right. He minds walking down on his own but, being on his own as he crossed the triangle & the triangle feeling quare lik, a bit, as he stepped down off it. He'd've known about triangles in them days even, a bit anyhow, *isosceles* & *equilateral* he'd've heard about at school, sure, & even if all that $a^2 + b^2$ stuff was still all Greek to him, it wasn't as if it was a right-angled triangle anyway. Naw, at most it would've been an isosceles maybe & he'd've stepped onto it at the top & come down off it at the bottom, the equal angles either side of him. An' aye: it felt a bit quare, he thought nothing of it at the time just.

Eleven or twelve Mass, it would've been. Daylight definitely. He'd've arrived after the rest of them but, must've worked his way in along the kneeler, the rest of them letting him as—tucking his bum in—he squeezed his way past. Well up the chapel they were, he minds, to the left facing the altar.

What he minds most is: even before the readings, someone was letting off. He looked along at Sean who—if it *was* him—wasn't letting on, who, if anything, was too far away but. Annette—right next to Liam, he minds—seemed blissfully unaware. The smell was something rotten but, seemingly. He looked round, he minds, Liam, to see who else it could be. He couldn't see it being the mother & father & two weans in front of them—they were too well dressed. Couldn't see it being the old woman wi the white hair & black mantilla either but. The list of suspects ended there, or: he got no further forward wi it, more lik, cos *This is the Gospel of the Lord* the priest was suddenly saying & *Praise to you, Lord Jesus Christ*, they all responded—Liam 'n' all.

Everyone had just sat down again & was trying to get comfortable before the sermon started when he realised, Liam, it wasn't coming & going, the smell, that it was there constantly & that that ruled out a phantom farter. That's when the feeling on the grass came back to him: as he was about to step down off it. An' that's why he was suddenly pushing himself back & sneaking his foot forward & though the kneeler was still down still & blocking his way, he managed to angle his foot to examine his sole. Annette, he made sure, didn't notice.

The sight that met his eyes explained everything: dog shit, he'd stood on buckin dog shit, the heel of his left shoe was lacquered in it. The dough for a cake it looked lik, or for fairy cakes, chocolate fairy cakes, cept wi grass—if grass was what that was—running through it. Naw, firmer than that it was. Aye: lik the mixture they used for Chelsea Bars more lik, that was the colour it was, but not as tough but, not as plasticiney. An' to rub it all in: now he knew it was there, the smell was even worser. Now he could actually see the shit, the smell was buckin rank, the worst thing being: there was no escaping it.

He shifted again in his seat to fish for a hankie, couldn't find one but, not in his right pocket & not in his left pocket either. He let on to sniff before he nudged Annette.

'Have ye a kleenex on ye?'

Annette shook her head.

'Gaun ask themmins for me. My nose is running!'

Annette tried: 'No one's got none,' she was soon reporting back but. 'Ciara has her own just.'

'Tell her to gimme it—I'm *desperate*!'

Ciara the wee love's hankie was passed along the pew. It looked alright: a bit snottery, not too snottery but, not too disgusting. Any snotters there had been had dried in, must've.

Liam let on to use it. Annette, he could see, was waiting—lik Ciara was wanting it back. He shook his head. 'Naw, let me keep it. I'll need it sure,' & she went back to listening to Father, what he was saying about the *age of reason* & the wee ones' First Communion next Saturday, their preparation for it, their First Confessions during the week there to purify their souls.

The priest's words, in Liam's case, were going in one ear & out the other just. Trying to work out, the weeboy was, sure, what to do wi the shit. Looking at the amount on his sole still, he couldn't imagine a single hankie doing it, one hankie on its own being enough lik. Naw, he doubted it. Doubted it very much. An' knowing the priest would be down lik a ton of bricks on him if he as much as bent down, he waited a good while, until well after the collection, before thinking of trying even.

Kneeling down for the consecration they were when he risked his first swoop. *Shite:* he knew right away he hadn't been on target, it wasn't a clean sweep. He'd a kleenexful of shit alright, there was more still on his shoe but & the dollop of shit now filling his hankie would hamper any folly-up. A way of folding it—he'd have to find some way of folding it, or of wrapping the hankie round itself, before he could even consider another attempt.

A friggin disaster, his second go—using the bits that were clean still—was. He should've known, should've realised, the youngfella: first time trying this or not, ye shouldn't expect to lift more shit cleanly wi a hankie full of a first lot. Shitty hankie or not, he'd hoped but to cup it round the mush, then fold the second lot in on the first. He hadn't a hope in hell, needless to say. When it came to the bit, didn't he miss some of the second lot; some of what he did manage to lift went over his fingers & to top things off, the buckin thing tore. There was shit now on the outside 'n' all. Shit all over the crumpled edges.

'I need another hankie!' he whispered to Annette, knowing—wi it in this state—there was no way he could just abandon the first, drop the first at his arse just.

'I toul ye: no one's got none,' Annette tried to tell him.

'Naw—*ask* them!' he pleaded. 'I'm desperate!'

Another hankie made its way along; Sean, the wee bugger, had had one all along. Again, it wasn't bad. Again, it wasn't that snottery. Again, any snotters had dried in, must've. Liam bided his time, waited for a quiet moment—*Take this, all of you, and eat it* it was, he reckons. Folks' heads would all've been bowed by that stage, sure, their fingers tapping their chests as the bell rang for *This is my body which will be given up for you.* That, or: *This is the cup of my blood.* At the second *Do this in memory of me* at the absolute latest, anyway, he used hankie 2, the weeboy, to deal wi the worst of the rest, saving some of No. 2 to wrap up hankie 1. He didn't as much as blink, apparently, the bugger—joined in for *Christ has died* even, *Christ has risen, Christ will come again,* when their cue came to *proclaim the mystery of faith.* It was straight into the *Our Father* after that, then *Peace be with you* & he didn't want to even think about it even, Liam: the germs on his right paw going—*Nalsowiyou!*—onto Annette's right paw &—*Peace be with you!*—onto the family in front of them's paws & from there—*Nalsowiyou!*—onto other people's. It was soon time to kneel again, fortunately, & before he knew it, they were all going up to receive. Seven, at least, they must all've been right enough then, the O'Donnell weans, at the time. Making Liam ten or eleven maybe.

He can't tell you what happened next, the weeboy, or: how it happened the way it did, more lik. Way they were sitting, he'd've been the last out of the pew & up for Communion. Whatever way the queue went but, way the traffic stalled or whatever, he was second in line coming back. Only wee Bernie was ahead of him & sure enough: she made, God love her, to go into the same pew, Liam but got hold of her in time.

'That's not the one!' he hissed.

She looked at him—as ye might imagine—baffled.

'We were further back!' he lied.

He could tell, to look at her, she wasn't convinced & pushed ahead just.

Bernie, it seems, hesitated but then just followed just, despite the rest of them trying to call them back. There was a bit of discussion alright, a bit of confusion, one or two of the congregation, granted, might've noticed something. Then the rest of them followed too but 'n' all.

For the first time since Mass had started, Liam could now relax. The pew wi the shitty hankies was at least three in front. A St. Vincent de Paul man or a Knight of St. Columba would find them after Mass maybe. The Union of Catholic Mothers, more lik, the next time they came to clean the chapel. For the time being anyway, the smell—thank God—was gone so it was & wi God's holy help, they wouldn't get caught. Naw, they'd leave at the end just—lik any other week. The rest of them & him would get their arses out quick. Quick, not too quick but & no one would notice.

Sure enough: *The Mass is ended. Go in peace*, the priest was soon saying & the congregation had hardly got *Thanks be to God* out, a response Liam always thought sounded wild cheeky, when the organ struck the final hymn up.

> *Fai-ith of our fa-a-thers li-vin still,*
> *In spite o dungeon, fire & sword,*
> *Oh how our hearts beat high wi joy-oy*
> *Whene'er—*

At the end of the first verse, the priest & the altar boys genuflected, then turned on a sixpence & stepped off the altar, the priest holding back to let the weeboys go first. Liam watched them sail along the rail & into the sacristy. As the priest's back vanished, the green of his vestments a rectangle, sort of, Liam nudged Annette. It was time to go. Annette, in turn, whispered to the wee ones. They hesitated a bit maybe, aye. She'd to nudge them & motion to them a second time, for sure. In the end but, they done what they were told but & went.

the troubles (for you)

1.

little tinkers! as weans, we'd creep up behind you—and to see if you could hear, tinkle-rattle gran's brass milkmaids from the fireplace. sometimes you'd catch us: grab one of our paws somehow. you didn't do nothing but. nothing happened to us. we'd build castles just. warm. if warped. shifting, piling, palms. face down. from the bottom to the top.

2.

the first time we went back, *over home* for the summer, you sat, silent, as ever watching, from that sunlit dented wheelchair. now looked out but onto barricades: armoured cars & tanks & guns, weeboys & youngfellas throwing stones, & soldiers *wi a mother too, somewhere, god love them*, behind gran's garden hedge.

   that night, behind blinds down for the rosary, I wondered were you *feart*, lik me, or oblivious. aisling, I mind, hearing the shooting, telling us but it wasn't, then racing out to shift her car, wide of the hug that you, crying out, offered—or wanted.

3.

fast-forward twenty years & they carried you upstairs one day—to see your mother in a box.

   people didn't know whether you *understood*. reported but that when you came back down, you were *vexed* alright.

enough to make your heart

Season 1971–72

It felt like Christmas had come early. First Liam knew, his da was tugging his toe.

'Surprise, son!' he whispered. 'Get up 'n' get on you quick! We're going to the football!'

'What, *Parkhead*?'

Liam could hear himself how excited he sounded.

'Naw, they're away this week in Dundee. C'mon, get up 'n' get on you like a good youngfella. We need to leave soon.'

Liam waited for the door to shut, then jumped out. Sean & wee Cahal, he could see, were out for the count still. Room was that cold, he was hugging himself as he hopped round, looking out his clothes. Even pulling them on, he was shivering.

He hoped to God his mum had the fire lit.

Sure enough: she was kneeling in front of the fire, a big double-page out of the paper up against it, when Liam got downstairs. *The British Army is smaller than it used to be*, the huge big advert read, *but so is the world.*

There was a hint of a heat if ye went close.

'Mornin, Mum.'

'Mornin, son.'

The trick wi the paper was a good one. Liam loved the way it turned gold as the flame started to take. You'd to watch it didn't catch just. Soldier wi the helmet was in big trouble if that happened.

His mum & dad were talking bout how come he was going to see Celtic.

'Bring your boy,' Mr. McCool had said, his da was saying. 'He'll be company for my boy, sure.'

'It's not fair taking one 'n' not the other but, Liam,' his mum objected.

'I can take Sean another time,' his da said just.

'See 'n' enjoy yourself anyway, son!' his mum said as they left. She slipped him a new 5p.

It felt strange: heading out wi none of the rest of them up yet. Felt great but too: him & his da, the two Liams, heading off together.

They took the big green Zephyr & parked behind the Hibs.

Liam—wee Liam—had never been in a bar before. It was mainly empty tables, wi empty & half-full tumblers & ashtrays in front of people but—where there was people. One or two seemed to know his da.

'Pint of cordial, Liam?'

'Aye, John, please!'

Barman'd started to make it before he'd even asked.

Orange went in first. Liam watched the colour change as black-currant was added.

'Lemonade for the boy, maybe?'

'Aye, give him a bottle of mineral, John, thanks. What do you say to Mr. Higgins, son?'

'Thank you.'

The bar was beginning to fill. Some of the other men had Irish accents too. His da & him weren't the only ones. Some of the other men said aye, they were going to the football, they weren't all but. Ye could see themmins that weren't wished they were.

Was a good while before anyone Liam's age appeared. When they did, they crowded round a table across the room.

'Gaun over 'n' join them,' his da kept saying. Liam wouldn't but. Not when he didn't know a single one.

He played wi his tooth that was coming out instead. Was still playing wi it, his tongue footering away, when the McCools turned up. That youngfella was over to the others like a shot.

Suddenly they were bundling onto the bus. One minute his da was going to the toilet &, not wanting to be on his own, Liam went with him. The next, they were bundling on.

'Come on, O'Donnell! Trust you—always bloody last! Can ye no hurry up thon father o yours, son? What kinda example's thon to set the boy, O'D?'

There was a buzz about the bus as they left. Liam recognised the obvious bits of where they lived in Scotland, but not much more but. He asked his da how long it would be. His da didn't know. The man across the aisle didn't either. He leant across, all kind: 'We've left in plenty of time anyhow, son. Don't be frettin.' The man laughed. 'Yir daddy here might even have time for a pint!'

'What—you don't drink? Pioneer, are you?' Liam heard as he drifted off in his own imagination.

'That you playing wi that tooth again?'

Liam nodded.

'Want me to pull it?'

He nodded again.

His da's finger & thumb went into his mouth. Liam ignored the yellow colour—tried to, anyhow—& the taste & smell of it. His da rocked the tooth. Liam could feel it resisting.

'It's not ready to come out yet, son, 'n' I don't want to force it. I'll try again later.'

Liam sat there just & wriggled & wriggled it, his face against the cold of the window sometimes. It got to the point the poem he'd learned in St. Eugene's wouldn't give him peace—the wobbly-tooth one.

They were crossing a river when a man appeared. He stood over them wi a cap full of toty bits of paper, folded up tight. It was the *sweep*, the boy said.

'Final score, is it?' his da asked.

'Naw, first goal-scorer for a change.'

'You choose, Liam. Let you choose—'

'That your boy?'

'Aye—my eldest. He's Liam, too.'

'Pleased to meet you, son. What age are you?'

'Ten!'

'Ten?'

'Eleven in March, he'll be. For secondary in the autumn.'

'Many others ye got?'

'Six. Another two weeboys and four weegirls.'

'Jaysus, man!'

His da opened his ticket & humphed.

The man laughed. 'Who've ye got?'

'Evan Williams!'

'The goalie! Ah well—ye never know. Maybe it'll be an o.g. D'ye want another one to be in wi a chance?'

'Not wi luck like that I don't!'

We *HATE Ran-gers 'n' we HATE Ran-gers*—

Singing had started already.

'Don't know what's brought that on!' his da said. Then but, he spotted the boys at the lights.

We are the Ran-gers HAT-ERS!

The Wranglers ones leapt out of their seats. Charged across the aisle to give the Proddies the vicky. Scary, it was. Specially when them other boys laid into the glass wi their fists. Least, over in Derry, the soldiers waved back if you wavved nice.

Soon, the singing was that loud ye'd've thought the match had started.

'Mon the Cellic!'

Most of them said the name lik it had no T in it.

Before long, they were giving it all the *grand-old-team-to-play-fors*. For once, they kept up wi each other.

WHEN—ye KNOW—the HIStorY—

Liam knew the words 'n' all. Was too shy to join in but.

enough to make your heart go oh OH oh OH

His da wasn't. Looked at him as if to say, Wha's wrong wi ye?

ANimals SAY

WHAAAT the HELL do we CAARE

His da fancied himself as a singer.

a SHOW

'n' the GLASgow CELlic will be THERRR.

Singing was frightnin enough now, would be worse still at the ground but. Ye'd to wonder why the other team showed up even.

The roars o them—

Liam always thought it felt lik, sounded lik, they could kill someone.

Eventually, they gave their so-called singing a rest, thank God. Kinda roads they were on, there was no one to taunt anyhow. At most, they brandished their flags & scarves at other supporters' buses. All the ORANGE BASTARDS got shouted, whether it was Rangers buses or not.

'Aye, they're not the only ones, sure,' his da explained. 'Some of them wee teams are just as bad.'

Mr. McCool came up to speak to his da.

'Have ye met my Kevin yet, son?'

His da said he hadn't.

'Away up 'n' introduce yourself. He'll be delighted to meet you.'

When Liam wasn't for moving, his da said his tooth was bothering him.

'Never mind—the Tic'll take your mind off it. We're goney stuff these boys theday, son! Where's your scarf anyway?'

'Not got one.'

'Not got one? Ye want to get yir daddy to get you one!' Mr. McCool turned to his da. 'Ye should get him one, Liam. All the other young fellas have them.'

'Who d'ye think Big Jock'll pick theday, son?'

Liam panicked. How was *he* supposed to know?

His da said something for him again.

'Who's your favourite player then?'

That was easy. Lennox. Bobby Lennox. Ever since the double he got against Falkirk. Wee Jinky was a close second. The rings he dribbled round folk.

'And can ye name me your favourite eleven?'

Liam couldn't.

'That boy o mine can. Obsessed, he is. Nothin appears in the papers he doesn't cut out. You should ask him to let you see his scrapbooks, son!' The man turned back to his da. 'I get him the catalogues wi the wallpaper samples from my work 'n' he sticks in everything he finds. I'll get you one, too, son, 'n' give it to yir da here to give to ye.'

'That's kind of you, Feargus. What do ye say to Mr. McCool, son?'

'Thank you.'

They got there eventually. Dundee was the furthest Liam'd been in Scotland. Wasn't as if he saw much of it but—two grounds on the one street & that was it.

Was Tannadice they were going to, not Dens Park. His da joked about making sure they got the right one. 'Ye wouldn't want the match to start to discover it wasn't!'

Mr. McCool laughed 'n' all. 'Aye—magine ye were stood there wonderin was that a new away strip Celtic were in?!'

A fair number of buses parked where they parked. Whereas Irish accents tumbled out of their bus, the Hibs bus, Scottish accents piled out of the other ones. It was all the didni-widni-kidni stuff Liam de-tested. All the effin bees 'n' all. It could've been Japanbloominese ye were hearing at times. To listen to them, ye wouldn't've known these boys had any connection wi Ireland, that was for sure.

Most of the men descended on the pub. His da said the two of them wouldn't. They'd head on in & choose their spot just.

The embarrassing bit came next: his da would never pay for him. Insisted on lifting him over. Always a struggle it was & Liam al-ways got stuck. Was worse still when Sean was there 'n' all & their da needed help. Thon shivery feeling as a stranger's hands went in under your arms—

They got in & climbed the steps.

He loved this bit, Liam: the anticipation as you headed up the steps. Then: the immaculate green below. It perfect, normally, till the match started.

What was noticeable this time was: the atmosphere wasn't as good. Tannadice, compared to Parkhead, was a ghost town. At Celt-ic Park, they'd be playing records. "If You're Irish." Or "Hail, Hail."

"You'll Never Walk Alone" too, of course. Sixty thousand scarves held aloft.

His da lifted him onto a crush barrier & stood behind him. Liam leaned back, knew not to cuddle in. If it stayed like this, he'd have a brilliant view. He knew from other games you could have a perfect view to start wi—then other folk would come but & blot it out. It wasn't fair. By that time too, it was always too late to find another place.

The ground was filling up. United fans were getting their songs in while they could. Would be a different story later.

Teams were read out. The fans booed one lot, cheered the other. 'No surprises there!' his da & Mr. McCool agreed.

'Naw, nae surprises there, eh?' the guy next to them gave it.

A huge cheer went up. Drownded out what the guy said next. Players were running on.

'United haven't read the script, Liam,' Mr. McCool was soon saying.

They'd the cheek to score first even.

His da & Mr. McCool looked at each other. Was Partick Thistle goney be, the League Cup final all over again, looked lik. All the effin bees the men around them were giving it. Singling out the goalie they were. His da'd to call them to order.

'Mind the language, lads—there's boys present!'

'Aw—sorry, Jim. Aye, nae borra. Sorry, big man!'

They reached halftime without an equaliser. Liam couldn't believe it. There'd been a few near things in the goal-mouth below & it was all he could do to remain on the barrier. The ball hadn't gone in but. United might even've scored a second.

It was a long cold wait at the interval.

'Don't worry, son,' Mr. McCool said. 'A different story in the second half it'll be.'

That didn't make Liam any warmer but, as he waited to be lifted again. Talking to someone about emigrating from Derry his da was. Scores from the other grounds didn't help either: Aberdeen were up there challenging still.

Second half started. All the action was at the far end now. It was all Celtic. Was hard to tell who was doing what but. Was the ball going in or not.

Crowd behind Liam was straining to see. There was so much leaning forward & falling back, he wasn't safe on the barrier. His da'd to keep telling folk to spare a thought for the boy. It kept happening but. Soon the weeboy was so scared, he hadn't a hope of concentrating. Didn't help that the men round about him were baying for blood.

'United are hangin by a thread, Liam!' Mr. McCool said. 'Like your tooth, son!'

Then Celtic equalised.

'CAESAR!'

Liam felt himself being swept off the barrier.

'Big McNeill!'

Took both his da & Mr. McCool to catch him.

His da was livid—'Youngfella could've cracked his skull open!' Fans were too busy celebrating but.

'One each!'

'M'ON THE TIC!'

No way was Liam getting up again after that. He stayed down even though he couldn't see. There was gaps between the men's bodies alright. They closed but, every time the ball went near the box.

Another four goals went in—Hood, Connolly, Murdoch, Hood again—Liam saw buck all but.

'5-1! Are you pleased wi the score at least, youngfella?'

Liam tried to say he was. Really but, for the last half hour, he'd been interested in nothing but his tooth.

They hit the road. Only stopped for fish 'n' chips. Perth was the name of the place. In the freezing cold, the steam off the food was something powerful. Heat made Liam's tooth scream wi agony.

'Eat wi the other side of your mouth then,' his da said.

After that, the journey dragged & dragged. There was nothing to look forward to. If he didn't see much on the way up, he now saw less in the dark, Liam.

He felt a sharp pain sometimes when he forced the tooth wi his tongue. When that happened, pressing against the window seemed to help. The cold would take his mind off it.

Two hours later nearly, he was still sitting there: poking & wriggling. Felt lik a crunch sometimes, it did. Then suddenly, it gave. His da hadn't to pull it.

Liam showed his tooth to Mr. McCool.

'Will ye be leavin it out for the Tooth Fairy?'

Was the first Liam'd heard of any fairy—though he knew about under the pillow.

'Don't know about that,' his da said. 'He's had enough—all he's getting—today.'

Youngfella didn't care but. He was so browned off he wanted home just.

** 2 **

Day it all happened, Liam'd been out wi a ball—ball he got for Christmas—up round the corner at the garages. No one else was out so he'd spent the afternoon, once twelve Mass & the dinner were over, kicking the ball at the doors.

He knew himself he was getting better. It felt great when he got a rally going, the ball hitting the door, then dropping down the slope, falling for him. He could feel himself shaping up, posing nearly, as he shot & shot & shot & shot at goal.

He kept going even when it started to get dark. Wi the street-lights on, it felt like a midweek game, sure. Floodlit.

Felt so good, was only needing the toilet had taken him home.

'There's three dead in Derry,' his mother said when she saw him.

'Is there?' he answered just.

He felt lousy. There was nothing he could say but. Was lik the times his mum would tell him, 'Your granny was sayin Tony Devlin died yesterday.' Or: 'That's Bridie Breslin dead.' He'd feel sad, sort of. All he could ever say but was 'Did he?' just, or 'Is it?'

The names meant nothing to him, that's what the problem was. His mum, realising sort of sometimes, would say, 'You must mind Tony Devlin? Man who ran the butcher's next to the newsagent's? Married onto your aunty Mary's people?'

'Naw, maybe you wouldn't,' she'd end up saying.

Was only him she asked, too. She never asked the young ones.

Liam wished he *could* remember. Instead of being a dead loss.

'There's five dead now,' his mum said when he came down again. 'Did ye wash your hands?'

'Yeah,' he said, racing out.

It was still bothering him but, as he looked to see who else was out. Ciara & Annette were playing wi them clacker things. Sean was nowhere to be seen. Boys next door were playing kerbie, so Liam sat & watched.

The number went up to eight. Then eleven. Then thirteen.

The Derry ones were phoning Mrs. Henderson's. His da still wasn't in so his mum took the calls. Came out each time to tell them.

'The rumours are true,' she announced at one point. 'Bout the killings in Derry, I mean. There was even a bit on the news there.'

'They haven't put a figure on it. Your uncle Dermot says it's all round Derry but there's thirteen dead. Thirteen dead 'n' a whole lot injured.'

Liam looked at her just. None of them knew what to say. He could see the shock too, sure, in the girls' faces.

At some point later, his mum came out of the Hendersons' & assured them the O'Donnells were all okay.

Jesus. It hadn't even occurred to him! Liam, when she said it, realised.

Her own family were all okay 'n' all. None of them had been on the march.

Some of their uncles & cousins on the O'Donnell side had been but they were all home safe but, she told them. Their uncle Dermot was just off the phone to say they were all home safe. Their daddy had got hold of Dermot 'n' all. Had phoned the Creggan from a phonebox.

When he got home from the Hibs, their da, you could tell from the look on his face it was really bad. You'd've thought, to look at him, someone in the family had died.

Now Liam felt even worse. Bout not realising how bad it was.

It was no time before Mrs. Henderson was at the door again. His da took the call this time, apologised for any inconvenience. Mrs. Henderson insisted but it was alright.

Turned out Dermot had phoned again & John Hume had read out the names from a bit of paper. There was twelve names, thirteen dead but. Folk weren't sure who number thirteen was. Could be one of two people.

The weans were all in their beds, of course, when *News at 10* came on. They could hear Big Ben but up through the ceiling, your man Reginald Bosanquet doing the headlines.

For once, the weans had been good & went up. Was as if they knew to. Sean was the only one to act up. Ciara & Annette were soon shooshin him but, urging him to be good for their mammy & daddy. Wasn't there thirteen dead, they said.

It was no time before they could hear their da 'n' all. Raging he was. Calling the soldiers for everything. Their mum they could hear trying to calm him.

When Liam went down for a drink, his da called him in.

'Mere 'n' see this, son.'

He didn't need to be told, Liam: the man on the TV wi the balding head, was Eddie Daly. The Eddie Daly his da had gone to school wi. Father Daly now. He was waving a white hanky, Father, & the boys behind him were carrying someone.

'Jackie Duddy, that is. Dermot toul me on the phone. Seventeen years of age! Jackie Duddy's his name. And Father was shouting "Don't shoot! Please don't shoot!" trying to get him to an ambulance.'

Jackie Duddy. Liam knew instantly it was a name he'd never forget.

He remained sitting.

His mum & dad were *letting* him, he realised at some point. Were letting him stay up. He listened to the army boys being interviewed, his da blowing his top. Then listened to his da & his mum trying to take it all in. Trying to piece it together.

Thirteen dead. Six from the Creggan alone.

The next night, when their da came home, he was livid.

They all knew at work he wasn't long over, he said. Not a buckin one but had had the decency to ask was his family all okay? 'For all they know, one of my brothers could've been shot!'

'They're all Catholics too. Each 'n' every one of them. Did they ask about Derry yesterday but? Did they buck! Not a single one!'

'That's the Scots for you.'

Their da stayed in that night, something he never ever done. Even wee Cahal commented.

Their mum & him were running through the names still. Trying to work out which Gilmore it was. Which Nash. Which McDaid. There were two by the name of McKinney.

It wasn't just grown men. There was seventeen & nineteen & twenty-one year olds—which made it even harder. Ye had to work out who they might be connected to. Whose youngfella it could be.

Liam listened to the names being repeated, over & over. It was goney be another list you'd have to know by heart. He could tell already.

They'd a name for number thirteen now. Boy's family, God love them, had been told it wasn't him & it turned out it was.

Liam's mother & father kept coming back to Jackie Duddy. They never shut up about Jackie Duddy. Bout Father Daly carrying him. Trying to get him to an ambulance. Having to wave his hanky to stop them getting shot.

Fr. Daly who his da knew from when they were schoolboys together.

** 3 **

The first home game again, after that, was the following Saturday.

The funerals had taken place in the meantime. Dermot had described on the phone for them what people had felt: all them coffins, all laid out before the altar.

Their mum & dad hadn't given over—even here in Scotland even—bout what everyone was calling Bloody Sunday. They went on & on about Bernadette Devlin punching Reginald Maudling. Bout other ones setting fire to the British Embassy in Dublin.

It showed you how serious things were.

Things were *bad* gettin.

There was demonstrations in America 'n' all, sure.

Devlin was expected in Glasgow on Friday night. Woodhallside, or something.

They'd seen the letters to the papers too. One, in the *Scotsman,* insisted the Ulster Catholics in Londonderry lived no distance from the border. *So,* the boy asked, if they didn't go, didn't move across, if they preferred to be second-class citizens in Northern Ireland when they could be first-class citizens in Eire, *did that not tell you something?*

Their da flipped when he saw that. Was writing in, himself, nearly.

The Saturday was a Cup game. Against Albion Rovers.

Sean was looking to go. Still hadn't been for when Liam had got to Tannadice. Their da wasn't having it but. Their mum didn't say nothing. However much she felt for the weeboy, it was a non-starter, she knew. He knew it was a bit twisted, Liam, something in him felt pleased but—specially when Sean got joined for asking once too often.

'I said NO, Sean, 'n' I'm not telling you again! It'll be a cuff round the ear ye'll be getting. Do ye not realise there could be aggro? It'll be no place for youngfellas—Parkhead—today.'

Mr. McCool turned up at half one. When he saw Liam, he said his Kevin said hello. Didn't say much otherwise.

Then he minded the tooth. Liam'd forgotten, himself, until Mr. McCool mentioned it. His tongue felt for where the wound had been. Marshmallowy, it had been, really soft. Coppery-tasting. Now but, it had healed again.

'Are you satisfied, weeboy?' their da asked when he came downstairs again. Talking to Sean, he was. 'Hasn't Mr. McCool left Kevin behind 'n' all? I hope you're satisfied now?'

He turned to Mr. McCool. 'Do us a favour, Feargus, will ye, 'n' tell my two Parkhead's no place for youngfellas today!'

Liam drew him a look as if to say: He doesn't have to tell me! Wasn't me was pestering ye!

'That's right, boys,' Mr. McCool confirmed. 'Yir daddy's right. Yir better off at home theday, Sean, son. Ye never know what could happen, sure.'

He turned to their da. 'I hear there's an International Socialist march in Glasgow planned. Ye ever heard o them boys, Liam? The International Socialists?'

Their da said he hadn't. He'd heard about the sixteen arrests outside the Bernadette Devlin rally the night before but. An' about a boy called Pastor Glass who'd led a counter-demonstration. There was a photo in the paper. Liam'd seen it 'n' all. *The People's Democracy*, one placard read, *is a Marxist Plot*.

'Have ye got the petitions?' Mr. McCool asked as they headed out.

'Too right I've got them.'

At quarter to four, Liam tuned in for the halftime scores, then listened to the second-half commentary. Sean joined him. It was okay: Celtic were two up; the Rovers weren't at the races.

The goals rolled in. 5-0, it finished. Callaghan got two. Macari, Deans 'n' Murdoch, one each.

The boys couldn't wait for their da 'n' Mr. McCool. Would be great if Mr. McCool had time to come in. That way, they'd hear more. Would hear how Dalglish & Macari were doing—the new boys.

When the two men did return, their two faces were tripping them. Even Bridget commented.

'What's wrong wi yous? I thought yous would've been pleased. The two boys here were followin it on the wireless.'

Their da shook his head as if to say, don't ask. He was browned off about something, ye could see it.

'They wouldn't sign our petitions, Bridget, love,' Mr. McCool explained.

'Aye—they call themselves Celtic supporters!' their da just about roared. 'And the buggers wouldn't sign our bloody petitions!'

Mr. McCool was nodding away.

'They stand on them terracings, week in, week out, singing all the songs, calling themselves Celtic supporters,' their da continued, 'calling themselves *Irish*—would they lift a pen but to put pen to paper? Would they buck!'

'Language, Liam!' Mr. McCool tried to say. 'Cool it in front of the youngsters, mucker.'

Their da wasn't having it but.

He turned to their mum. 'I tried to reason with them, didn't I, Feargus? Thirteen dead, I said. A whole lot more injured. Thirteen innocent people murdered—'n' you won't put pen to paper?'

'I tried to plead wi them. It's true, I said. The world press has got hold of it, sure. Like in October '68, I said. All them foreign journalists, cameramen, witnessed it, captured it, have put the English to shame . . . Wasting my breath but, I was, love.'

'Liam's right, Bridget. Hardly anyone signed. The boys at the Hibs did, but not the ones at the ground. For all their songs, for all they wave the tricolour, all ye got was: *naw, mate—ah widni want any bother wey the polis.*'

'Ye wouldn't've credited it, love,' their da said. 'Thirteen dead 'n' they were scared they'd get in trouble. Well, it's the last bloody time they'll see me. "If You're Irish," ma arse! Green white 'n' gold, ma foot. That's the last buckin time *I'll* go anywhere near that friggin shower—I'm tellin ye!'

Way he said that last bit made Liam look at Sean.

Aye—

Sure enough—

Ye could tell from the look on his face: wee bruv knew he'd be a long time waiting, if he was waiting for their da to take him now.

somewhere down the line

For Pablo

It was half twelve & if Tom Nolan didn't get his rear in gear & out of the house soon, his wife would be getting suspicious. He couldn't believe he was doing this, this week again. Here he was: wi a gale blowin & it chuckin it down outside & whether he wanted to or not, he was about to head out into it. Sarah—passing through—was like that: 'You're goney miss your train!' She'd a face on her. 'Or are yous no goin for a pint first?' she follied up wi, on her way back in from the bin.

That *yous*, as usual, riled him. What was it prevented her from saying his big mate's name? The pint, cos of her, was always *beforehaun*, too. Case of home after the game, it was, or risk—

'So are yis or aren't yis?' she was suddenly insisting.

'Naw—aye, we are!' he answered, quick.

Lying through his teeth, of course, he was.

The bus came right away. He peered out the window as it drove into town. The occasional flash o black & white soon became a flood. Saints fans—from the odd one near the Infirmary, to the packs around the Piazza—were aw over the joint. Partying already.

The bus pulled up in the tunnel & he got off.

'Ye aff tae Parkhead, big man?' a voice at the stop asked.

Young boy from work, it was. Tom, barely stopping, acknowledged him.

'Ah am, aye.' (Lying again.)

'Big Ron no goin theday?' the boy cried after him.

'Ahm meetin him in Glasgow.' (More lies.)

He took another soaking as he dashed from the shops to the station. Guys were having a jar, he saw, in what used to be the Post Office. He was tempted alright but had to press on.

In the station doorway, a couple o auld dears were battling wi their brollies. One was putting on a plastic scarf.

ALL TRAINS IN ALL DIRECTIONS MAY BE CANCELLED was the notice that greeted him when he finally got to enter.

It was thon way: ye didnt know whether to buy a ticket.

Other folk were.

'Central, please,' he said when his turn came.

'Return?' the boy asked.

'Naw—single!'

He'd left the motor at work. If the trains were like this but, he'd go & bloody get it.

In luck he was. Within ten minutes or so, a train did come. It was jam-packed wi fans. Rangers were in Motherwell today & these boys, fae Ayrshire, were on their way there. Three, sitting doon, clocked his scarf.

He undone it—to get the good of it later. The scarf was part of the pretence. Part of the act for Sarah's benefit. He'd need to watch. Diddy that he was, he'd nearly left it behind. Truth of the matter was: he'd been doggin games aw season. Him & his big mate hadni been for months.

A "mature student" the new lassie was. Half Ron's age. Tom hadni met her, had seen a photie but. Through in Edinburgh she stayed. Mr. Jackson knew which side his bread was buttered on alright. Week in week out he was over, now, in the east. Even his beloved Tic were oot the windae. Waste ae a good season ticket if ye asked Tom. Waste ae *two* good season tickets, to be exact—cos Tommy-nay-pals wisni goin either. Was going through the motions just. Sad but true but: whenever the Tic were at home, he was dragging himself out & driving intae town—passing by Ron's even, as if he was going tae collect him. His usual route. Their usual schedule. Anything, rather than admit to Sarah that Ron & Moira had separated. Anything, rather than give his wife yet more ammunition against him.

Since September, this was going on. To begin wi, he *did* go alone. It had been strange: reaching the ground, wi'out going first for a pint but. Been strange: getting to their seats & Ron's remaining empty. Been strange: no having his mate there to discuss the various incidents. He was on nodding terms, of course, wi the folk round about. The string of priests in K. The schoolteacher friends, who sat to Ron's left. The mechanic & his girlfriend, who sat to Tom's right. The boys, in M, fae Belfast. They knew each other to see, aye. It wisni the same but. No the same as having Ron there.

'Yir big mate no well at the minute?' the mechanic had asked eventually. Tom had invented some illness. 'Yir big pal still no any better?' the same boy had inquired when they played Falkirk. That's when something snapped. When his wee excursions had started. To the pictures, say. The sauna. Museums. Or the Clyde—

He hadn't the energy for lying.

Didni matter who was playing. He gave the fitba a bye.

The train pulled into Central. It wisni raining, ye could see it had been but. Plus: it was blowin a gale.

The scarf stayed on as he walked down Union St. Nae intention o going, but his scarf was stayin on. Some o Sarah's friends could be shopping, sure.

As he turned onto Argyll Street, he was nearly splashed by a bus. The place, to his dismay, was chock-a-block. He hated this street at the best of times. The further ye walked along, the more he loathed it. Some o the stuff ye were expected to buy was unbelievable.

The thing that kept him going was the Tron. He knew the bar fae years back. Knew he'd be safe in there. Relishing the thought already, he was: of having a read, a bite to eat, & tuning in to the chit-chat.

Chisholm Street. The scarf came off, needless to say, as he took the sharp right. He stuffed it into his jacket. Zipped the pocket shut. Last thing he wanted was a corner pokin out.

His favourite waitress approached.

'Hi,' he said. 'What's the soup of the day?'

'Lentil 'n' bacon, sir.'

He approved. Nodded. 'I'll have some.'

'Followed by the burger, right?'

'Please,' he said.

He'd told her a previous week about seeing it featured on telly: how his mouth was totally watering even just watching. His mate going AWOL had been the perfect opportunity. Now, it was a regular habit, getting. His treat to himself on match-days.

He demolished both courses.

'No coffee—just the bill?' the waitress checked.

Fact she remembered made him smile. 'Just the bill, thanks, yeah.'

Back out on the street, he made for London Road. The wind hadni calmed any. Garbage was blowing aw over the shop like the snow in they wee glass things. He walked on & walked on, keeping his head down, a hand across his eyes to shield them. He wisni caring who seen him now. The general direction was Parkhead, *basta*. His scarf back on, to complete the picture.

More & more fitba colours there were now: guys falling out o pubs; younger boys in flags, chanting, singing. When the wind let them, the younger lads especially were givin it laldy. Their sheer aggression could be scary. Even when Tom was a regular, he'd not felt part of this. Strange, that: how ye could be walking the same street, wearing the same colours & yet part of ye didni feel part of it. They'd agreed to disagree on this, him & Ron. He wisni one for singing, Tom. Wisni one to roar. A *yesss* when Celtic scored wis the height of it.

He walked on. Nearing Glasgow Green, chanced a side street. Two lanes of traffic were coming at him. Taking his life in his hands, he'd be, if he insisted on trying tae cross. The obelisk up ahead, at least, was what he wanted to see. He crossed the road at the end. Ye couldn't see the river. It had tae be straight ahead but—between him & aw they tower blocks. Along to his left was where he was heading. The People's Palace. His favourite museum. Still a bit of ground to cover. Out of his bloody mind he was—way the wind was hammering aw they bushes & trees. He continued anyhow, walked on regardless, his head firmly down against the gale.

Seeing him arrive, an attendant he knew to see opened the door. The guy, Tom minded, was Celtic-daft.

'Thanks, mate,' he said. 'Think the Tic'll do it theday?'

The auld boy looked at him. Seemed to mind.

'God, aye,' he said. "We'll *cuff* this lot, sir!'

He headed for the Winter Garden first. For once, the cafe did little to relax him. It was cosy in here & the coffee was cracking. The storm had totally rattled him but. A grown man shouldni be doin this! Pathetic, was what it was. He was like a kid skipping Mass again, 'cept instead of having to find out who said Mass, what colour of vestments he wore & what the Gospel was about, he now had to know who scored. The order the goals came in helped an' aw. 'Two up, were they?' 'Consolation goal, was it?' Red cards were like second collections: ye had to know there'd been one.

There was a nephew wi his uncle at the next table. The boy tucking into a cone. Uncle enjoying his pastrami. If what had happened hadni, his own wee young fella would be this boy's age now. He winced as the look on Sarah's face came back to him. For a moment, even felt sorry for her. It wasn't a bit of wonder she was the way she was. Wasn't a bit of wonder the shutters came down.

The wind howled again & rains rattled the glass. As wet as it was wild again, it was.

Weather, last time, had been better. Inspired, he'd sat out on the steps even & sketched the carpet factory. The basic facts he knew fae his school days. That it was based on a palace in Venice. Or resembled a carpet laid oot on the Green. He'd quite enjoyed drawing it & the result hadni been bad. He'd binned it on the way to the car but. He'd never have heard the end of it, sure, if Sarah'd found it. Doodling. *Doodling*! An' worse still: lying—*lying* to her—about attending the flippin football.

Outside wisni an option theday. No in this weather, it wasn't.

He fished out his book. The book he should've been reading already. Wisni as if he could read back at the house

Flight to Afar. He was back into it in no time.

He reached the endae a chapter & checked his watch. Twenty-five minutes gone, maybe.

The auld guy caught his eye as he crossed to the Gents.

'Still nil-nil, sir.'

Tom nodded just.

Inside, like the last time, he refused to rush. Studied the tiled border as he dried his hauns. Strange place for Shakespeare, right enough.

'Nil-nil still,' the auld yin confirmed when Tom passed him again. 'No long tae hauftime now.'

'Killie holdin out then?' Tom half-asked, kind of, no wanting to say nuthin.

A wedding party was arriving as he approached the main staircase. Chinese—fae here but.

He climbed the stairs, his thoughts beginning to focus on the story he'd spin Sarah. Nuthin each, if it stayed that way, was a dawdle. 'All over them!' he'd give it. 'Couldni put the baw in the net just!' No that Sarah was one bit interested, like. A few token comments was aw he needed.

Reaching the first floor, he cut through World War II. There was a staircase in the corner, he minded, that took ye up to the second. A kid, he could hear, had packed the evacuation case right. The train was choo-chooing: the sign he'd got the items right. The air-raid siren had been triggered by someone an' aw. Tom could hear the mother as the family raced for cover. A wean protesting, 'Ahm readin, Mammy!' He could just imagine them aw: huddling in the shelter. The mother, the granny, the grand-wean, the dug.

First time he'd sat in there himself, there'd been an empty Irn Bru can. Part o the display, he'd decided. They must've had Irn Bru, even in they days. An auld dear, in wi her grand-weans, had put him right.

He passed the steamie, the dairy. Climbed the stairs to the top. The display, needless to say, hadni changed any. First thing you clocked was political stuff. Slogans. Banners fae marches. This time an' aw, the SPANISH WORKERS FOR DEMOCRACY thing gave him a bad conscience. Folk fae here had died in Spain, he knew. He'd meant to find out why, but hadni. Other things he did know about. The ANTI POLL TAX UNION and PEOPLE'S MARCH FOR JOBS, for instance. It was stuff—at a pinch—he could've, should've, been part ae. No him but. Too wishy-washy. Always had been, always would be. These days, he hardly said boo to Sarah forgodsake. Ne'er mind boo to any cunt else.

He headed through the back. Last time, the top floor had been shut & he hadni seen the Banana Boots. Together wi the portrait of the Big Yin, they were probly his favourite exhibit. He loved the memories he had: *Parky* on the telly in the seventies, his ma & him watching. Him, at thirteen, bitin his cheeks. Trying tae make out he didni get the rude bits.

There was that crackin auld typewriter an' aw. The pile of books beside it. Glasgow books. Aw stuff they hadni done at school.

He checked his watch again. Final whistle couldni be too far off.

Was still nil-nil, he took it.

He headed back to the stairs. The attendant was staunin in a balcony kind of area. Tom strolled over to join him. You could see the Winter Garden! Looking onto the café, they were. Down onto the plants.

The wedding party was taking photos in what little light there was. The different permutations posing before the palms.

'It's still nil-nil, sir,' your man confirmed. 'Defence is holdin out still.'

Tom wandered off again.

Next thing he knew, he was back at the air-raid shelter. There was no one else around so he parked his bum. He quite liked it in here. It was tight, cramped—room for six, he'd read. A world away, of course, fae CELTIC PARK: the two-tier stand, the floodlit stadium, the screen wi live coverage. There'd been a time when aw that thrilled him. Sixty-thousand others, the night sky above him. Now but, it done his head in. It wisni him. He couldni hack it. Even the folk they'd chatted tae. Don't go askin him why. Somewhere down the line, summit had changed just.

It wis partly, maybe, the thought his da came here. His granda too. Baith, of course, were deid now. Or just the realisation he could never go wi his boy.

Flight to Afar—

To kill the remaining time, he took his book out. *Ahm readin, Mammy!*

He was so engrossed he must've missed the announcement.

A lady suddenly was tapping his shoulder. 'That's us closin, sir! Unless you want to spend the night in there?'

She follied him downstairs. The attendant acknowledged him as he left.

'Finished nil-nil, sir! Disappointing result, eh?'

'Right enough!' he said just. 'Right enough!'

The Chinese party follied him out.

Darkness had descended more or less. The rain had stopped—which was summit, at least. There was something like a mist, a haze. The fountain and the obelisk were lit these days. The lamps just underlit the haze, though. There was a touch of the Hounds of the Baskerville about what he was stepping out intae.

Dark & misty or not, the wedding party was onto its outdoor shots. Tom looked on, intrigued. The photographer's flash shattered the darkness—once, twice, a third time. Tom joined in the laughter & the people seemed to include him. The happy couple waved even. The light was poor but it felt like the bride was looking at him but. Was looking to test his heart or summit. He remembered his own wedding suddenly, the sincerity he'd spoken his vows wi—& something, he couldn't've said what, went through him. He didn't want to lie any more but, he realised. But nor could he be truthful right away.

He fished oot his scarf & put it on. Looped it over once & pulled it tight.

The wool—for that split second—choked him.

'Time ye were gettin home, boyo!' his head told him.

a day out
April 1974

The alarm went off. Liam groaned but reached but to knock it off before it woke his brothers. Now he was at secondary, he was used to getting himself out. Today but was Sunday & last night they'd got staying up—to watch Eurovision. The Royaume-Uni had blown it, he minded as his feet hit the floor. Not that he cared. The song was dull. Olivia's wasn't as good as Cliff's last year.

POW-er to ALL our friends . . .

He'd got up at the first ring, knew he'd half an hour to make the bus. In Paisley for ten sharp, they'd to be.

'The coach'll leave without you if you're late!' the Scout leader had warned. 'I'm delaying it for no one!'

Conscious of this, Liam pulled his clothes on, quick.

'Don't forget my rock, bruv!' Sean muttered, hearing him slip out.

His mum—the star!—had tea & toast ready when Liam got downstairs.

'Thought you were lying on?' he said.

'Didn't want you going all the way to Edinburgh on an empty stomach,' was all she said.

She busied herself around the kitchen as he ate.

'That you off?' she called when she heard him in the hall. 'Here! Don't be telling your daddy but!'

She slipped him two bob, to add to his 50p.

'Thanks, Mum,' he said & hugged her.

Eddie Cassidy was approaching the Steps as Liam left the house. Heading for the same bus, they were, obviously.

'Mind-reader!' they both shouted. Then: 'Jinx!'

Eddie got in a split second before him so it was Liam was the jinx.

Thinking there was no rush, they took the Steps calmly. There was no point in breaking your neck when there was no need to. As they crossed the main road but, they could see a double-decker leaving Bobby, Alan & Keith's stop.

'Take it ye watched the Song Contest?' Eddie asked as the bus approached.

Liam nodded. His family'd watched it every year since Dana won. (They still lived in Derry at that point.) Some of them had even cheered Lulu on even, the year before that.

'Some song that won it, eh?' Eddie said.

'Not half!' Liam agreed.

'They two birds were gorgeous!' Eddie laughed.

Liam'd noticed the blonde girl's bum 'n' all. Wasn't one for dirty talk but.

'A half to Paisley, please, mister!' he said instead to the driver.

They went up to the top deck to join the other three, Liam toppling all over the place wi the movement of the bus. Drew Campbell, it turned out, had joined Bobby & his crowd. Bobby's brothers were there too. George, his big brother, was sitting up the front wi his wee brother, John. He should've realised, Liam realised. It was the Scouts they were going wi & not the school, sure.

'Whit ur *you* daein here?' Eddie asked Drew Campbell.

'Slept at ma gran's last night,' was all the answer he got. Maybe cos of the slagging Drew'd been given the last time.

Forget Eurovision—Bobby & his crowd were talking about the Cup. Hearts & Dundee Utd had drawn—so Celtic didn't know yet who they'd meet in the final. Not that it bothered Drew. 'Athletic Madrid oan Wednesday's the big wan anyhoo!' he was maintaining.

Eddie, the only other Tic fan, agreed.

'Aye, forget the Scottish Cup—by bedtime oan Wednesday,

we'll've completed oor hat trick o European Cup finals!' he predict-ed. 'We'll dae the job at hame! Bet ye any money!'

'Doubt it!' Keith—their only Ger—objected.

'Wha' d'ye mean?'

'Wan-nil against Arbroath yistirday an' ye think it'll be aw over eftir the first ninety minutes against the Spaniards?!'

Ye could see Keith was getting cocky again, now Rangers had a bit more faith in themselves. For him, winning on Saturday had been a *crucial step* towards Europe. He went on slagging Celtic, the others letting him, till he made the mistake of insisting Rangers could still be champs. Even the Saints fans among them pounced on him. Bobby laughed it off, insisted Celtic would be. Alan, another Buddy, decided to top Bobby.

'Tell ye somethin else, pal,' he taunted. 'It'll be Hibs or Aberdeen that finishes second! No yous lot!'

Keith wasn't one bit amused. 'Least we've got summit tae play for—unlike you lot! Second Division dross!' he sneered.

The bus pulled in at their stop & they walked through the Piazza & across to the GPO.

The single-decker outside it had to be theirs. Sure enough: they soon spotted the leader, Cameron, chatting away to the driver.

Other boys, already on, roared & hammered the windows as they approached.

The driver was raging.

'That's enough o that!' he shouted. 'Any mair o that an' yis'll be gaun naewhere!'

'Tell them!' he insisted, turning to Cameron.

Cameron told them.

Liam let everyone else board first. It was his way of avoiding a red neck. Of letting the rest decide who was sitting where.

The seats up the back were taken. They'd to settle for nearer the front.

'Don't worry—on the way back, we'll get the back seat!' Alan—would-be hardman—muttered to Bobby.

Cameron was counting them. 'Nineteen. All present and correct!' he announced, from up the back. 'We can go, driver!'

He was still on his feet as the bus pulled off. Leant on the back of the seat he'd be sitting on to talk to them.

'Edinburgh it is, then!' he announced wi a big smile.

They all cheered & he sort of put his hand up to stop them.

'It goes without saying I want you on your best behaviour!'

The cheering stopped.

'Promise?'

'Promise!' some of them promised.

'I'll tell you more when we get there,' he said. 'But basically, what I've arranged is: a visit to the Bridges, a visit to the Commonwealth Pool, and a quick stop at the shops on the Royal Mile.'

'You all brought your togs?' he asked.

The others nodded.

'It's okay, I haven't forgotten you can't swim, Liam,' Cameron assured him, looking in Liam's direction.

A hand went up. 'Derek's forgot his, Cameron!'

'Is that right, Derek?'

Cameron shook his head in despair. 'There's always one!'

Then it was lik he'd changed his mind: 'Derek will be company for you, at least, Liam!'

'Okay, first stop the Bridges! More from me when we get there. Now sit back and enjoy the journey!'

The journey was boring. There was nothing to see, but then they knew that from previous excursions but. The Catholics among them, anyhow. Bobby, Alan, Eddie, Drew, & Liam had gone wi the school, sure, in Primary 7.

The school went, always, to the castle & the zoo. Today'd be something different, at least.

As Liam relaxed—saying hi occasionally just to ones who passed—he noticed everyone round him had settled already. Most of the others were sitting in pairs, chatting away to their neighbours. Lucky him had *two* seats—behind Bobby & Alan. Bobby was being good about it: had already turned round to see was Liam alright? Bobby was a good pal, got. Kind. Helpful. Always making sure ye weren't left out. Was him who suggested Liam join. That he go some Friday night. 'It's a non-denominational troop,' he'd explained. 'A whole bunch fae our school goes though.'

The bus crossed a bridge, then continued on its way. The windows might've been filthy, Liam forced himself to look but. It was a chance to see more of Scotland, sure. It was only a couple of years since they'd immigrated.

Wa-Wa-Wa-Wa—Waterloo . . .

Eurovision! The winning song was going through his head, kind of. That's what was going through his head.

Liam wished he knew the words. The song was a cracker. A future party-piece, for sure. A good job it was 'n' all: he needed something better than flippin Cliff. His gran hadn't been impressed. 'He done alright, aye. I still don't see why he couldn't learn the Irish song but!' she'd said in front of him to his da last summer.

Something else came back to him & he had to laugh. Last night had been funny, right enough. He could still see them all sitting round the living room—his mum, his da, the weans—all determined to be quiet. He'd had his tape recorder set up, bang in front of the telly. Annette had hers on 'n' all, the PAUSE button down between the songs. The rest of them'd agreed to sit at peace & shut up. From half nine till quarter past eleven, silence had been golden—apart from the results bit & the gaps between the songs. The only interruption had been their da going for a pee one time. 'Away 'n' scratch yourself!' he'd objected when Ciara protested. 'Wha' d'ye take me for?' It was a good job it was just the Greek song just.

Normally, on long journeys, like during the sermon at Mass, Liam would replay goals in his head—or the most impressive snookers from *Pot Black*. That many memories from last night were popping up but, a top five was needed. He decided on the positions, then the DJ in his head took over.

At 5 were his sisters: looking for translations, knowing he'd started learning French. The words to the Belgian song were hard but. Same went for Monaco. France had pulled out cos of Pompidou dying.

At No. 4 was his da, disappointed at Ireland coming seventh. 'Suppose they can't do a Dana every year!' he'd eventually conceded eventually.

At 3 was the voting—the usual carry-on. The reason why Ireland gave the English so few votes but wasn't cos of the Troubles. It was cos their song always topped the charts beforehand & folk were sick hearing it.

Just missing out on the top spot, at 2, was the Dutch song. The one wi the barrel organ. The younger weans had had a soft spot for it: the big boy wi the beard & twinkle in his eye, the pretty Dutch girl accompanying him. 'Mouth & Macneal—what kinda name is that?' their da had laughed. 'Ye wouldn't want to be called a mouth in Derry!'

And straight in at No. 1 was ABBA. A-B-B-A. Brilliant, they'd been. Plus the great surprise of them suddenly switching to English.

Aye, he'd definitely learn the words, Liam decided. They'd it on tape back at the house, sure.

The journey was dragging.

He twiddled his 50p. It was one of them ones wi the hands—to mark Britain being in Europe.

'Penny for them, wee man!'

Liam jumped. 'What?'

It was George, Bobby's big brother. 'Penny for your thoughts!' he repeated, laughing.

'They're not worth it,' Liam said just. He didn't want to admit it—he was thinking but of buying ABBA *and* Mouth & Macneal, once the singles came out. It was his birthday, sure, in a couple of weeks & he could probably afford both. A toss-up, it was, between the Dutch song & the new record by Wizzard.

George—older than Bobby, obviously—was too mature but, too political, to discuss what singles to buy wi. 'I've no seen ye since the Election, pal,' he began, kneeling on the free seat. 'No properly, tae talk tae . . .'

Liam nodded, minding how they'd spent the day up at the Protestant primary, asking everyone who passed how they'd vote.

'You must've been pleased wi the result,' Liam said. 'Labour getting in . . .'

'Definitely!' George agreed. 'I just hope they *stay* in. We could have anither election oan oor hauns afore we know it, ye know . . .'

'Is it not supposed to be every four years?'

'Yeah—it's a minority government this time though. An' Wilson's got all that private-land-deals stuff comin at him. Also: inflation's up nine percent since January, an' the engineerin workers are threatenin tae go on strike. The social contract might no be worth the paper it's written oan!'

Liam wondered how George knew these things. Bobby was the same. Maybe it was their da. Their *faither*, as they called him—who always seemed to be constantly changing jobs. One minute, he was a car worker. The next, a shop steward. The next, he'd be back making cars.

Chuffed his pal's brother was taking time to talk to him, Liam let George continue just. On about the Budget next, he was: how the increase in family allowance would soon be felt. These were changes for the better, he kept saying. Liam didn't comment—was just glad he knew now who was bloody who. Healey, wi the eyebrows, was the Budget man. Wilson, the guy wi the pipe.

'Cameron's comin!' George eventually interrupted himself. 'I'll need tae get back tae ma seat . . .'

'What age are you now, George?' Cameron asked as he squeezed past, making a big joke of their bums rubbing.

'Sixteen in June!' George answered. Ye could hear how proud he was.

'I'm only twelve. Thirteen this month but,' Liam volunteered when the leader looked at him.

'Everyone else already *is* thirteen,' he added, since Cameron was still studying him. 'Or going on fourteen. I skipped Primary 2—that's the reason.'

Cameron seemed to ponder this, then leant down to confide in him. 'Do you know what saddens me, Liam? No? I'll tell you since you're a clever kind of boy. Year after year, Liam, I see boys getting older alright. It's rarely the case I see them getting wiser though.'

Liam didn't know what to say to that. It was like his da's 'Aye, you're getting big, alright: big in the buckin mouth!' He never had an answer for it.

The radio suddenly came on. Liam, when it happened, realised he'd heard the others asking for it. "Seasons in the Sun" was playing & the same ones were pleading now for the driver to change the station.

'Whit's wrang wi Terry Jacks?' the driver laughed, la-la-la-ing along.

Their one consolation was: the record was finishin. Even if he didn't turn over, the song would come to an end. Liam had to laugh. An' he agreed wi the others: the song *was* lousy. The worst No. 1 this year. Not a patch on Sweet or Mud. Or Alvin Stardust. Or Suzi Quatro.

"Shang-a-Lang" came on & the bus went mental—though the Rollers were for weegirls. Gary Glitter's "Remember Me This Way" had them singin along 'n' all. Cameron'd to go round, tellin them to sit down: the driver could have to brake, sure.

The next couple of songs were quiet ones, fortunately. Stuff Diddy Hamilton played & housewives liked. "The Air That I Breathe"—The Hollies. "The Most Beautiful Girl in the World"—Charlie Rich. The different ones round about Liam started talking again.

When the news came on, it was as if the other boys stopped listening. Liam was listening but.

'It is alleged in a West German magazine to appear tomorrow that Her Majesty the Queen is regarded as a target by the IRA. An interviewer for the *Spiegel*, based in Hamburg, recently met six of the seven members of the IRA Army Council, it is claimed, at a secret location in Dublin. The IRA, insisting that it is *at war* with an *enemy*, sees Her Majesty as a *legitimate target*, the magazine reports.'

Liam—prepared for anything, suddenly—looked to see what the reaction was. Would they turn on him? Then he minded his Scottish accent now but. That he'd lost his brogue. Only the boys he went to primary wi knew he was from Ireland originally. Others wouldn't know unless they told them.

When he managed to concentrate again, the newsreader'd moved on to Eurovision. 'The nineteenth Eurovision Song Contest, held in The Dome in Brighton last night, has been won by Sweden. The winning song, "Waterloo," was performed by a group—ABBA. The two couples who form the group have been celebrating their surprise victory. The bookmakers' favourite, the United Kingdom entry, "Long Live Love," performed by Miss Olivia Newton-John, came a disappointing fourth.'

The DJ on after the news decided to play the winner.

'This is the wan ah wis tellin yis aboot!' Liam heard Eddie telling others. 'The two lassies are total rides!'

Liam was popular today alright! George was bouncing up to him again, this time wi Mark McCarthy—another patrol leader. Drew, looking younger than normal, trailed behind them.

'Is it true what Drew's tellin us, Liam?'

'What?'

'Bout you choosin yir subjects for Third Year?'

'Aye. It's just an indication but. We still don't know who'll be creamed off.'

'I know that fae Bobby, yeah. But is it true whit Drew's sayin aboot *you?*'

'That I'm dropping Science? Yeah!'

He could've mentioned that Bobby wasn't, wasn't keeping the promise they'd made in First Year. He didn't but.

'An' did they haul ye up to the office, right enough?'

'Yeah—'

'*How?*' Mark barged in. 'Whit were they sayin like? How'd they no jist let ye?'

Liam could see the older boys' amazement. An' that Drew was glad he was giving them confirmation.

'*Do you realise you're throwing away your future, boy?* was the main thing.'

The other three howled at this. Mark repeated it even, doing a great impersonation of Mr. Quigley.

'An' whit did *you* say?'

'Well, ye know it's a double column? Physics AND Chemistry. Or Art *or* Greek *or* German AND Statistics?'

'I seen that oan Bobby's form, aye,' George replied.

'Well, I said I want to do Greek!'

'An' how'd ye justify that?'

'I said I wanted *a second modern language.*'

The older boys recognised the quote. A *second modern language* was *an option*. Nearly everyone done Science but.

'An' did they pressurise ye, like Drew's sayin?'

'Yeah, Quigley got the Marks Book out when I tried to insist I was rubbish at it. It was in front of the Head 'n' all, when they hauled me up to the Office. Quigley showed them my A's in all the tests. I insisted but that I never *understand* Science. "So how do you explain these A's, boy?" Donnelly suddenly asked—like he smelt a rat. I learn the summaries by heart, I told him. The ten-point summary at the end of every chapter. That's where the teacher gets the questions.'

George & Mark were loving the fact he'd tripped the teachers up.

'Classic!' Mark laughed. 'Straight flamin A's—claimin ye cannae dae it but!'

'They tried to get me to *think about it*,' Liam went on. 'Boys wi the intellectual ability to do Physics and Chemistry should choose Physics and Chemistry, they said. Art and Modern Languages are for pupils who lack that ability.'

Mark repeated this 'n' all—imitating Donnelly this time.

'An' they didnae manage tae force ye?' George checked.

'No. I just kept repeating I wanted to do Greek . . .'

'An' whit did Donnelly say?'

'When I wouldn't give in, he kept shaking his head just. Eventually, he said that that was that then: if I was determined to throw away my future, to go ahead and throw it away, but not to try and say I'd not been warned.'

'So yir daein Greek?'

'I'm doing Greek!'

'Put it there, pal!' George said.

Liam shook the hand George held out.

'An' don't be worryin!' George continued. 'Once ye get tae the Academy, it's aw new teachers. Quigley & co. hivnae a look in.'

Mark shook his hand 'n' all.

'George is right! Well done, pal!' he said.

Drew, Liam could see, was jealous.

Cameron was wanting their attention. The Bridges were coming up.

They got off at some kind of viewpoint. It was dry & sunny, a wind was blowing but. Cameron tried to show them just the Road Bridge first. Ye couldn't help but, of course, but see both. The tenth anniversary of the opening of the Road Bridge was this year, which was why they'd come. Our Queen and the Duke of Edinburgh had opened it, Cameron made a point of stressing. The way he said "*Our* Queen" didn't escape Liam.

'It's a suspension bridge—the longest outside America and the fourth-largest in the world!' Cameron continued, proudly. 'The central span alone is over three thousand feet. Add the two side spans and the approach viaducts—and you've some overall length. Twenty million pounds we're talking, boys. That's what the total cost was.'

'How did people get o'er there before?' Eddie asked.

'They swam!' Drew said, sounding right sarcastic.

Cameron looked at him, then said: 'By ferry. There was a ferry service. I was on it once!'

'Or ye could take the train, right?' Alan, serious as ever, chipped in.

'That's right. The Rail Bridge has been there a long time. It was opened in 1890, a decade or so after the Tay Bridge Disaster, if you've heard of that. Do you all know what a cantilever is?'

The boys hummed & hawed. Cameron wasn't about to tell them.

'It's complicated,' he said. 'Look it up at school. What you see there,' he pointed along to the Rail Bridge, 'are three *double* cantilevers.'

Whatever they were, cantilevers, Liam had to admit they looked good. The colour of them was crackin.

'It's a mile and a half long,' Cameron went on. 'The longest railway bridge in the world, back in 1890! Famously, it impressed the Shah of Persia even. Fifty-five thousand tons of steel you're looking at, boys. Over eight million rivets.'

'Some bloomin Mecanno set!' some smartass joked. Cameron frowned.

'Can I ask a question?' George asked.

Cameron nodded.

'Do we know how many *died*, buildin the bridge?'

'We don't,' Cameron conceded. 'Or rather: I don't!'

'But there were some?'

'I would think so. Yes.'

Liam could suddenly imagine them plummeting off.

'I bet ye guys died buildin the Road Bridge 'n' all!' George said, angrily.

Cameron didn't take him on. 'Speaking of the hard work that went into it: people say that if you want to paint the bridge and start at one end, that end will always need done again before you've reached the other. The work's never finished, in other words. It's a modern version of the Sisyphus myth.'

Alan sniggered. Bobby could guess why. 'He said "sissy fuss" or summit,' he hissed, 'no "syphilis!"'

Cameron must've caught the snigger too. Chose to ignore it but. 'Okay, boys. Have a wander round. A good look. Stretch your legs a bit. Then we'll drive on in to the pool.'

'It's some view, Cameron!' Liam said as the others wandered off.

'It is, isn't it?! I know someone who's flown into Edinburgh. The view's amazing, apparently, when you're still out over the water.'

There was a lot of talk of *Treasure Island* as they boarded the bus again.

'The inn the inn Long John Silver turns up in is based on is doon there!' Drew was raving to anyone who'd listen.

'Really?' Liam couldn't imagine it.

Cameron confirmed but that Stevenson, the author, had Edinburgh connections.

The driver was soon being asked to turn his tranny back on. "Waterloo" was playing—which got a cheer. Folk were already joining in at bits already. The brass & piano got your feet tapping. Aye, Liam now knew what he'd be spending his birthday money on. "Waterloo" and "Rock 'n' Roll Winter." It would be Wizzard, after all.

It was nice seeing the castle as ye entered into Edinburgh. It looked better from a distance, Liam reckoned.

Arthur's Seat was the name of the other bump you saw. The crags were smart too. Cameron told them about the glacier that had made its way through. Edinburgh might look totally dead, like a film set. The thought of a glacier cutting through it livened it up but.

Soon they saw the sign they wanted: ROYAL COMMONWEALTH POOL.

The boys jumped out of their seats as the driver parked up. Queuing in the aisle, they spotted Cameron lifting his swimming stuff.

'What—are ye goin intae the water wi us?' some of them asked, startled.

'Of course! Or did you think I could leave you unattended?'

'Magic!' one or two of them said. Others weren't so sure.

Cameron turned to Liam before following them in. Called Derek across before he spoke. 'See that hill ahead of you? That's Arthur's Seat—where it meets the Salisbury Crags—from this side! You could be climbing that, instead of sitting on the bus. It's perfectly safe. What do you think?'

'Ahm up for that!' Derek agreed, nodding.

Liam wasn't so sure, he'd no choice but.

'Just keep an eye on the carpark, will you?' Cameron asked. 'And come straight back once you see us.'

'Will do,' Derek promised. He sounded like he was glad now that he'd forgot his stuff.

The two of them left the car park, keeping an eye on the traffic. At the bottom of the road down, there was a fair bit of grass to cross before you started to climb. Derek set off, running. Liam tried to keep up, soon decided just to walk but. He always got a stitch when he ran. Knew he'd be quicker walking.

It was incredible: there was loads and loads of space here. An' it was lovely 'n' green 'n' all. The flat bit, especially. The slopes had yellow patches—stuff growing on them. Liam picked the one crisp bag blowing about up, so as not to spoil it. *Keep Britain Tidy*, 'n' all that.

There was a father out wi his boys & their kite. An' other people, walking. Some settled for down below. Others were determined to climb.

Arthur's Seat didn't look easy, exactly—but then Liam had never climbed before. The 59 Steps, or from Central up to British Home Stores, was the most he'd ever done. Looking at the slope, the tufts of grass, the bits of rock, he wondered how to get up it. There was jaggy bushes 'n' all—to make things harder.

They reached a bit where you could suddenly see water straight ahead—water wi an island in it. Over to your left was the castle. Liam stopped for a photo. The picture he took would make a really difficult jigsaw, he realised. Grass & rock just, on one side. The loads of houses round the castle, on the other. An' the sky, of course. Sky was always hard.

Derek, when they reached the steepest bit, took off like a goat. He was able to climb, standing, whereas Liam, afraid of slipping, was forever clinging on. The first few steps were easy enough, it soon got harder but & Liam could hear his breathing. It was lik he was dizzy, getting. Eventually—not before time—it got easier. Derek, he saw, had reached his target & found a place to sit. It looked good. Liam couldn't wait to join him. Derek surprised him, as he got closer, by encouraging him. He could've given him a pure slagging.

There was an empty Coca-Cola can between two rocks. Liam pocketed it.

They sat there, looking.

'Can't believe I done that!' Liam said.

'It'll be easier goin doon!' Derek assured him.

They looked at the castle. Derek drew a slanting line down from it—the Royal Mile, he said. There were ugly buildings too but. And if you looked far enough, you could see the bridges. 'Naw, no doon at the water!' Derek told him. 'Away o'er there, beyond they hills!'

'Are ye sorry you're not swimming?' Liam asked.

'No at all. No one bit! Ah *like* this kinda thing. Ah go bird-watchin wi my uncle Pete—The feathered variety!' he hastened to add.

The two of them sat savouring it, taking it all in. There was a silence okay, but it wasn't embarrassing but.

'Time tae head back doon! That could be them noo!' Derek eventually said, pointing.

Liam couldn't see what he was pointing at. Agreed it was time anyhow.

Going down was harder. Liam was really struggling.

'Yir makin it difficult for yirsel!' Derek tried to tell him. 'Try tae relax 'n' jist *go*. Yir slammin oan the brakes too much.'

Liam could see himself going down on his behind, if this continued. Ye wouldn't go head first if ye were on your bum.

At some point he could feel the difference—that it was safe to walk.

Nearby, papers trapped in what Derek called *gorse* caught their eye. Taking the look off the yellow they were, so Liam headed over to lift them. Derek was tight on his heels. Turned out it was magazines, stashed away by someone. Derek made a lunge for them when he spotted the titles.

'WOW!!!'

'What is it?' Liam asked. 'What are they?'

'Tell ye back at the bus!' Derek said, stuffing them into his coat. 'Jist don't breathe a word o this tae Cameron, right?'

He ran off ahead again. 'Come oan! We don't want tae be late!'

They could tell there was an atmosphere when they reached the bus. Cameron had a face on him. He clocked they were both back safe, didn't come up to speak to them but.

It was George who did. 'Had yous a guid time climbin?'

'Yeah—but what's wrong here? Why the faces on everyone?'

It was like George was telling Liam—but letting Derek hear too.

'Cameron's threatenin tae cancel everythin,' he said. 'We could be headin straight hame.'

'Why? Thought we were going to the Royal Mile? An' what about our souvenirs?'

'There's been an incident. Four of the Hunterhill lot seen Cameron in the scud. Naw, it's no that,' he added hastily, whatever way Derek reacted. 'They wee toerags were at fault. Tam Muir 'n' his lot thought it would be a laugh tae go intae the Adult showers. So they barged in an' there's nae doors, apparently—an' Cameron wis staunin there: bollock. Hunterhill mob couldni jist apologise an' be done wi it, o course. They went tae toon on it. Made a big laugh 'n' joke ae it. Bared their behinds, apparently. Cameron's mortified. Oot in the dressingrooms, he'd even asked us patrol leaders tae take the younger lads intae the Boys section while he got changed in the Adults bit. Tae make things worse: everyone in the dressingrooms— strangers an' aw—heard whit happened. It's a bloody shame.'

'An' everyone's goney be punished cos o that?' Derek asked.

George nodded. 'Possibly, aye.'

'Whit, like a hale class gettin belted at school?'

George nodded again—'We'll no forget oor visit tae the Commie Baths, wull we?'

He wandered off. Derek, disgusted, drifted off 'n' all. 'Ahm goney crucify that Muir wan!'

Liam headed over to Bobby & Alan just.

The Exorcist being shown in Glasgow was what they were talkin about: the stooshie surrounding it.

The instruction soon came to board the bus. They were all incredibly quiet being. No one had tried to swap seats even.

Cameron, they could see discussing wi the driver. The driver, back from the café, shook his head in dismay. He was completely agreeing wi Cameron, obviously. They were nearly finished talking, it looked like. Cameron nodded, then the driver, followed by Cameron, climbed aboard. The driver took his seat. Cameron didn't.

'I have an announcement to make,' he said. 'And I plan to keep this short. Due to some very immature behaviour, a breach of trust, an *abuse* of trust, which you all know about, no doubt, I've decided to cancel the rest of the programme.'

There were groans. Filthy looks were directed at the Hunterhill ones.

Cameron held his hand up. 'Silence, please. While it pains me to disappoint the majority because of the actions of a minority, the rest of the afternoon's cancelled. There will be no more sightseeing. No Royal Mile. There will be one final stop though. The driver has kindly agreed to stop at a gift shop. With the exception of four boys whom, I trust, I need not identify, you will be allowed to leave the bus and make your purchases. We'll then drive straight home.'

He sat down, almost, then turned to them again: 'Oh—and one more thing: when we get to Paisley, I shall speak to the four exceptions, individually. I trust they'll have something to say to me.'

He looked like it was unexpected. He got a round of applause but, Cameron. A round of applause from the troop.

Round of applause or not, there was disappointment in the air. Liam could feel it. He himself sat back but, feeling relieved. This way, he could buy rock for his mum & dad. An' Edinburgh Rock for the rest. Also: this way, they were guaranteed to be back in time for Mass. Today was Palm Sunday. An' when his mother & father had agreed to let him go, it was on the strict understanding he was back for seven Mass.

The shop the driver stopped at was a cracker.

Halfway home—Liam was munching crisps & talking to Bobby & Alan through the gap—Derek suddenly appeared & plonked himself down.

'Ahv your share o the money for ye, Liam!' he announced, brandishing a fistful.

Liam—who'd forgotten their find—looked at him just.

'Ah sellt they mags tae the older boys!' Derek explained. 'An' guess whit? They're bran new issues. Jist oot! They're pure lappin them up, up the back!'

Bobby & Alan were up on their knees lik a shot.

'Whit mags?' Alan demanded to know.

'Shoosh!' Derek warned him. "We don't want Cameron findin oot.'

Liam was looking at the coins. A fortune, it was. The sight of it was enough to scare him.

Derek whispered to Alan, in an attempt to shut him up.

'Whit? *Fiesta*? *PLAYBOY* 'n' all?' Alan repeated. 'Hidden under a bush?'

'SHOOSH, ah bloody said!'

Derek looked at Liam, then down at the money. Liam shook his head. Something was suddenly telling him the magazines were *dirty*.

'No, keep it, Derek! Was you sold them!' he said. 'I don't want any money! Honest!'

'But you foun' them!' Derek protested. 'Fifty-fifty's only fair!'

Liam refused again. Bobby was looking lik he understood the reason. Alan & Derek, but, clearly thought he was nuts.

Not that Liam let it bother him. He knew he was a stick-in-the-mud. Folk said so all the time. It was the Irish in him, was what his da said.

He knew how to stick to his guns.

Wasn't one to go along wi things just.

'Ye might at least've let us see them!' Alan—trying to sound big again—complained. 'I can't believe yis bloody sellt them!'

The look he gave the two of them was something else.

Liam ignored it. 'Naw, Derek, put the money away!' he urged. 'An' hurry up before Cameron sees ye!'

Cameron's name was hardly out of his mouth when he clocked the look Bobby was giving him.

'What?' he said, nervously. 'Why ye laughing? What's so funny?'

'Nuthin!' Bobby assured him. 'I'm not laughin! I'm just pleased to see you're learnin, pal. That's what it is: I'm pleased to see you're learnin!'

the way to a man's heart

Sean McNulty—part of him, anyhow—couldn't believe he was doing this. Drivin the length of Scotland, he was, to screw a bloody whore.

Was his big mate's doing, of course. Needless to say, wi a woman involved, was Andy who'd given him her number.

Goldie, she called herself.

The road was clear and he was making okay progress. Traffic was moving rightly, the drivers behaving themselves. A9 was notorious, of course—not that that stopped some cunts. Always some cunt there was who'd pull some stunt as dual turned to single.

Sean glanced at his mirror, clocked his ugly visog.

His two eyes were staring back at him.

A long way to go, Inverness was, for sexual fuckin intercourse. Andy swore by Goldie but. 'Ye'll end up thankin me! Bet ye any money!' he'd insisted. Same boy wasn't for saying what it was about her. Through the Internet he'd met her. More, he wasn't tellin.

Bottom line was: ye had to trust the bastard. Boy knew what he was talkin about. Free Love veteran, maybe. He was also willing to pay for it but. That's how he knew the things he did, he insisted. Ye didni learn they things fae wee Jean next door.

Aye, Andy'd been around, alright.

'Oor faithers screwed aroon in the war,' was all ye got out of him. 'Noo, it's oor turn!'

Our fathers did like fuck, Sean reckoned.

An' anyway: there was limits.

Was late afternoon, he hit Inverness. Found the street he was after. More a dead end, it was.

Curtains twitched as he reverse-parked at what was surely Goldie's door. The gate opened at the second attempt. Walking kinda awkward, he was, as he footed it up to the door. Was hard to be casual but, knowing *she* could be watching, *neighbours* could be watching, the *whole bloody street* could be watching.

G. FRASER was the name on the door. He doubted the G was for Goldie.

It opened before he could chap.

One look it took and he knew it was GAME OVER. He wouldn't be hidin the sausage, wouldn't be fuckin nae cunt. Goldie was no spring chicken.

'You must be Sean,' the woman said, eventually, when still he hadn't said nothing.

'Yeah, eh—Andy sent me,' he answered, sounding totally fuckin pathetic.

Andy, he knew, was into mature, this but was fuckin pushin it.

'So, you comin in, Sean, or you goney take root on my doorstep?'

'Naw, I'll come in.'

He needed a slash if nothing else.

'Mind if I use your toilet?'

'Upstairs, first on the right,' she said just.

There was a basketful of condoms on the windowsill. Next to that potpourri stuff.

Johnnybags apart, this could've been any bird's toilet. All that make-up stuff on the shelves & ledges. Flash-Domestos-Vim beneath the sink. Shower was still damp from the last time she used it.

A sign above the toilet asked men to sit down too. The wee cartoon guy had parked his arse on the floor. Was spraying all over the joint as he failed to hit the target. Fuck that for a lark, Sean thought, unbuckling his belt.

The cistern was still gurgling as he made his way back down. Goldie was in the kitchen, sounded lik. Hadn't made straight for the bedroom.

Peeling and cutting veg, she was, when he stuck his head round the door.

'Come away on in, Sean!' she said. 'D'ye fancy a cuppa?'

'Could murder a cuppa tea, aye—'

'You must have a hell of a drouth on ye—after all that driving, I mean.'

He sat himself down as she reached for the kettle.

A good arse she had on her still—he had to admit.

'Big pot of soup going on?' he asked. Partly just to say something. Partly being good in the kitchen.

'Naw, it's stews I'm making,' she answered. 'Irish stew.'

'You're jokin me!' he said. 'Christ, I'm buggered if I can remember my last plate of stews! I'd give my right arm for some!'

'You're welcome to stay, if ye like. Your big mate did.'

'I didn't mean it that way!' Sean said, embarrassed.

Trust Andy but, to get his feet under the table, he thought.

'There'll be plenty, sure,' Goldie insisted. 'And what we don't eat today, I'll have to eat tomorrow. And what I don't eat tomorrow, the dogs'll get.'

'Can I ask you a stupid question, Goldie?'

'Fire away.'

'*Are* you Irish? You don't sound it.'

'I am and I'm not,' she answered. 'I'm not trying to be funny. It was my mammy & daddy who came over. During the war. What about you? When did you emigrate?'

'Twenty-odd years, it is now.'

'From Derry, I take it?'

'Aye—how'd ye know?'

'You haven't lost your brogue.'

'So folk tell me. I was old enough not to, I suppose.' He paused, thinking about it. 'I take some stick for it too, right enough.'

'Well, don't listen to them. It's lovely, so it is.'

It was a compliment. Not said in a way but that could mean she was making a pass.

She interrupted the vegetable-cutting to pour him his cuppa. Caught him admiring her arse, nearly.

'I'll be with you in a minute, Sean,' she said. 'I want to finish this while I'm at it. How's Andy, anyway?'

'Aye, same as ever,' he said. 'Up to no good, as usual.'

He laughed to show he meant it in a friendly way. Despite what had happened some weeks back.

'He was good craic when he was up here, that's for sure,' she said.

'Aye, you can count on Andy for a bit of craic,' he said. 'Andy likes his craic, sure.'

They yapped a bit about Andy boy. Swapped tales of his various exploits.

'Bit of a lad, aye, heart of gold but,' was Goldie's verdict.

'Can't argue there: we've been mates a long time.'

'Well, I'm glad he sent you up,' she said.

That last bit was meant kindly enough. Just minded him he'd ruled sex out but.

A good while later, Goldie was chopping away still.

She was hardly in a hurry to get down to business. Or sensed, maybe, he wasn't.

Sean was watching her every move.

'You're like a bloody hawk!' she laughed.

'I'm glad to see you don't put sausage in!'

She looked at him, as if to say: eh?

'You don't put sausage in your stews.'

'Naw, you're right: I don't. What made you say that?'

'It's just: some folk in Scotland do. For me, it's a cardinal sin but. Sausage meat's bad enough. What I really can't abide but is folk cutting up what they call *links* and putting them in. The sight of bulging meat's a total turn-off. Once they're cooked, I mean—'

Goldie laughed. 'The things that annoy people!'

'Oh—sorry! I didn't mean to offend you!' she said, spotting his reaction. 'Anyway, you can relax: there's no sausage in my stews.'

'How do you make them?' he asked.

He was playing it safe, he noticed: sticking to safe subjects, to postpone the subject of sex.

'Well, to begin with, I boil a ham hock in the biggest pot I've got,' she said.

'I was thinking that's what I smelt.'

'Then I throw in the usual. Salt and pepper, to season it. Potatoes. Carrot. Onion. Bit of parsley maybe. The stuff you see in front of ye. And then I add the mince—'

'What kind?'

'I buy McGilvary's over here. There's nothing to beat Doherty's back home but. There's nothing to compare either, of course, wi a good Irish spud. The Scots can keep their tatties!'

'Mince balls or broken up?' Sean asked.

Goldie laughed again.

'Mince balls, I suppose, now you ask. For the reason: they're easier to share out. Not that there was any of that to be done, once the kids flew the nest and my man skedaddled.'

He could've asked about her husband. Didn't but.

'You sound like you're very particular,' she said. 'Are ye a bit of a cook yourself?'

'I cook a bit, aye. I had to, after my wife—' He interrupted himself. 'I take it Andy told you?'

'He did say something, aye. That was sad. Very sad—'

'I'm not bitter but. There's no point in being bitter. Anyhow,' he said, to get off the subject again, 'I make a mean potato fritter, if I say so myself. And if I've been lucky at the fishing, I know what to do wi the catch. I've a sister-in-law insists no one does salmon lik me. I've never ever made stews but.'

He paused, as if he was considering it.

'My mum made them, of course,' he continued. 'Both my grannies 'n' all. My Granny McNulty was famous for hers. Wednesday was Stew Day in her house. She collected her pension on a Tuesday, you see, and would buy all the ingredients, God love her, on her way back. She liked to cook them the evening before—leave them to stand overnight. Swore that made them taste better. One thing's for sure: the grandweans flocked to her door. Myself included. After school on a Wednesday, it was: no faffin around, and straight up the road to Mammy Nulty's.'

'It's got memories for you then?'

'God, aye! Memories galore. The smell of them cooking on the range. Your granny finally serving them. The way she ladled them out. Way they spilt over the plate. Way they reached an' filled in the edges. Way the grown-ups would be giving it: Eat roun' the edges, I'm tellin ye!'

Goldie laughed. 'I didn't listen either! Many's a time they scalded the mouth off me!'

Sean smiled. 'Did you ever eat a spoonful to discover it was stone cold? They were lik microwave food before their time, stews!' he joked. 'Stone cold at the edges. Roasting hot in the middle.'

She laughed again. 'You're right,' she said. 'I've never thought of it like that—you're right but!'

She stood up to fetch the mince. Was a half-pound packet just, he noticed.

'Fancy another cup before I start this?' she asked.

'That'd be great, aye!'

She put a refill in front of him, began to roll her mince balls.

To begin wi, Sean could've imagined her massaging him lik that. Then her palms got sticky wi the mince but.

'Don't worry—it'll wash off!' she assured him, seeing the way he was looking at her.

He finished drinking his tea while Goldie transferred the stuff. She did the veg first. Lik a work of art, it was: all beautifully peeled &

cut, stacked high on a beauty of a board. The smell off it was lovely.

'Can I give you a hand?' Sean asked as she made to lift it across.

'Naw, stay where you are, sure!' she answered.

That *stay where you are* made him realise what Andrew buckin Douglas would be up to by now. Andy'd be over pestering her. Would be pressed up against her, his trousers at his ankles, his fingers—

Goldie was seasoning the mince. A final shake before joining the veg.

One thing was for sure, Sean was thinking: if Big Andy was here, that mince would have no buckin chance. No dinner would go on till that randy shite had his way.

The mince was sitting proudly at the top. Would sink once the veg collapsed.

'Be right with you!' Goldie said. 'Once this lot reaches the boil, we can lower the heat and leave it—'

'There's no rush, Goldie, love!' Sean said. Not that he was sure what he meant.

She stopped to wash her hands again, this time using soap.

The aroma of whatever the handwash was made a pleasant change from the stews.

Moments later, she was standing behind him, vaguely massaging his shoulders.

She planted a kiss on his crown.

'So, big boy, you and me goin upstairs, or not?'

He was aware he was looking away from her. Of not having to face her.

'I'm happy as I am, to be honest,' he answered.

'This your first time, Sean?' she whispered. 'Wi a bad woman like me, I mean? It's just: you don't exactly seem in any rush.'

'It's only the first time since the last time,' he answered.

She laughed, thinking he was jokin.

He couldn't blame her. He'd thought he was jokin 'n' all.

Suddenly it was clear but, he wasn't.

Was the first time since the last time, right enough.

'No offence, Goldie—' he started to say.

He felt her almost seize behind him.

'Please don't take this personally, love—'

Any second now he'd get thumped.

'The two of us upstairs isn't going to happen but. Not today anyway,' he said, to cushion the blow.

She was considering her next move, it felt lik.

'Blame the conditions on the road—'

Lying through his teeth, he was. It worked but.

'Tell you what: I'll run you a bath, Sean,' she said. 'Then we'll see. You can still change your mind if you want to. Or eat a bite of dinner and go just. Okay?'

'Okay,' he agreed—relieved. Thinking: it was very decent of her.

A good—undisturbed—soak in Radox later, he returned to Goldie's table, wrapped in the chunky dressinggown he'd found on the back of the door.

'Did ye enjoy your bath?'

'Was great, aye!'

Emptying the last of a bottle of red into two glasses, she was, and smoking the last of a fag.

'Your health,' she said, handing him the biggest.

'—and safety!' he joked.

She looked at him just.

'Health & Safety!' he explained. 'A wee joke just!'

She gave a wee laugh. As if to humour him.

'D'ye fancy a plateful of stews, Sean? A spoonful, to taste your mouth, at least?'

'God, aye!' he said. 'I could murder a plateful.'

Between the long drive and the hot bath, he was now feeling in want of something.

You can keep the sex! he was thinking, retaking his seat. Great value this was, as it was.

The stews she put in front of him were a brown colour. Lik a wee tight perm in a hairnet. Weren't all runny and skittery, lik his Granny's.

'I put Bisto through them,' she explained, seeing the look he was giving them.

The Bisto must've thickened them.

'It gives them a bit of colour,' she added, when he continued to look uncertain.

'They can look a bit dishwatery otherwise, I suppose,' he agreed.

'Knife 'n' fork?' she asked. 'Or a spoon?'

'Spoon!' he laughed. 'Big wean, that I am, I'll take the spoon!'

He tasted a first mouthful—spooned up carefully from round the edges.

'To die for!' he declared. 'God—this takes me back!'

She smiled as she sat down to join him.

'Have you ever tried what the Scots call *stovies*?' he asked, once Goldie'd got herself settled.

'Yeah, they're not as good. That's why I make stews, when I do make them!'

'They're a mean and miserable version of stews, if you ask me. Wi whatever juice was in them dried up out of them. Is it any wonder a certain type of Scot looks the way they do? Anaemic!'

'Joyless!'

Goldie had to laugh.

He'd to laugh, himself. 'Naw, there's nothing to beat a good plate of stews!' he declared. 'These here are lovely!'

'I enjoy kedgeree, myself,' Goldie said. 'A plate of kedgeree's nice for a change.'

'Is that Scottish 'n' all?'

'Yeah,' she said. 'D'ye not know it? It's an East Coast thing, maybe. I'll make you some another time you're up.'

He took that as a positive sign: talk of a possible next time, despite his reaction this time.

'Kedgeree's wi rice,' she said. 'Rice and fish. Wi flakes of smoked haddock in among the rice. And a boiled egg maybe, or an onion, through it. The haddock colours the rice.'

'Sounds nice!' he agreed. 'I wouldn't mind trying it.'

'Come another time then.'

That sealed it: he was safe, he reckoned. *Hell hath no fury* wasn't at the races. He wasn't about to be hounded out of town.

'I must make you my Bavarian stew some time too then,' he offered, relaxing into their recipe talk.

'*Bavarian?*' she teased. 'Swanky!'

'Aye, I learnt it on holiday in Austria. Two types of meat. Three types of veg. All layered.'

'Sounds good,' she said.

'It is,' he said. 'It's great. An' dead easy. You fry up your beef 'n' pork, say, first—in separate pans, wi onions. Then you put the beef at the bottom of the stewpot, cover it wi half the veg. A layer of cabbage, layer of carrot, layer of spuds. All sliced. You season that wi salt 'n' pepper 'n' caraway seeds—'

'Caraway, eh?' she teased again.

'Then you do the same again, starting wi the pork. The remainder of the veg goes on top of that, three layers again, finishin wi the spuds. Add salt, pepper 'n' caraway lik before, pour a jugful of stock in, pop on the lid—an' you're off! Let it cook till the veg is ready. Let it do a bit more, if you want. Delicious, I tell you!'

'Sounds it!' Goldie agreed.

'It's even better reheated.'

He tucked into some stews before he went on. Just as he made to speak again but, she cut across him.

'Know something?' she said. 'Nothing beats cookin for someone, then sittin and watchin them eat it. One of the sexiest things in the world!'

'I think I know what you mean,' he agreed—but didn't take it further.

'What was it you were goin to say there?' she asked.

'Och, I was just going to mention a Russian variation. Borscht, they call it. Wi beetroot, it is. I tasted it once. The beetroot was hard work though, I thought.'

Soon as his plate was cleared, she was up to give him seconds. She didn't stop to ask first. He didn't try to stop her.

'It's lovely talking to you, Goldie, love!' he said.

'Likewise,' she said. 'Likewise.'

It was even easy talking to her, he noticed.

They cleared their plates, then Goldie started into the dishes.

'I don't like leaving them,' she explained. 'It's easier just to do them.'

She made him another cuppa to wash the stews down.

He sat drinking it, watching her—the arse on her again—as she pottered round the kitchen.

Now they weren't talking, Andy came back to mind. Sean could easily imagine what he'd got up to here. *Imagine* wasn't the word for it. More a case of *mind*. He'd still not forgiven the cunt for the stunt he'd pulled in Airdrie. Forget the sordid details of the build-up. Forget his running commentary in a *Kama Sutra* accent. What really took the biscuit was his appearance at Elsie's shoulder. Way, before you could've blinked, the cunt had joined them.

'When one lane of traffic turns to two, we call this position—'

Just as fuckin sickening was his gormlessness afterwards. Cunt couldn't see what the problem was.

'*You*, mate, should've left the fuckin room!' Sean had roared. 'Should've waited your fuckin turn *outside*!'

'You've gone very quiet!' Goldie said, reaching for a dishcloth behind him.

'Yeah.'

'Ye alright?'

'Yeah.'

'Want to talk about it?'

'Not tonight. Another time, maybe.'

That—while we're on the subject—was the other buckin thing:

Goldie here deserved better. The liks of Goldie Fraser shouldn't be whoring.

He wondered what it was that had her the way she was.

They'd only met. Something about her'd got to him but. No fuckin denying it.

Was right enough, what they say: the way to a man's heart is through his buckin beer belly. He was now even imagining coming back.

On that note, he rose.

Goldie was drying her hands, having finished drying the dishes.

'I'll need to be getting on me 'n' going, Goldie,' he said. 'It'll be touchin midnight as it is, sure.'

'Yeah, you've a fair drive ahead of you.'

'I'll just pop up 'n' get into my clothes!'

She stepped aside to let him.

Upstairs, he draped the dressinggown over the bath & for a moment stood there, naked. His eyes were staring back at him again. From the bathroom cabinet, this time.

The eyes of a guy walkin out on a pro.

The eyes of a guy who hadn't had his hole.

He gave himself a shake & reached for his gear—that neat 'n' tidy pile atop the basket.

One after the other, he pulled them on.

He tried to give her her money before he left. The tenners he'd counted in advance.

'No way! I'm not taking money off you!' she said.

'Take it, sure,' he said, trying to press.

Still, Goldie refused. 'An expensive plate of stews, that would be. Even including the carry-out!' she joked, pointing to the bag on the table.

Inside was a tupperware tub. Enough for a couple of dinners.

'Stews?'

'Stews!' she confirmed. 'Your Mammy Nulty was right. They'll taste even better tomorrow!'

'Tell you what, love,' he said, as a compromise. 'Play a book at Bingo for me!' He placed a fan of notes on the table. 'For as many Friday nights as that'll pay for. If I win, you can let me know, sure, an' I'll come 'n' collect my winnings.'

Goldie nodded her agreement. Smiled.

'Don't let it depend on a win, Sean. I enjoyed our chat too much. I enjoyed the Irish in you,' she added, seeing his surprise.

'And tell that Andy Douglas one to get his arse up here! Not to be a stranger.'

He was relieved she didn't suggest they travel together.

'I will. I'll tell him. I promise.'

She nodded, lik she was pleased.

'That us then?'

'That's us.'

'Could you do one thing for me, Sean, before you go?' she asked but as—his hand still on the handle—he was halfway out the door.

'If I can, love, surely, aye.'

'Would you just give me a hug just?'

'I'll give you a hug, certainly, love!' he said.

a trip to carfin
Spring 1976

'SOME'DY BRING ME UP THE TOILET ROLL!'

It was that wee shite Cahal again.

Liam ignored him.

'SOME'DY BRING ME UP THE TOILET ROLL!'

He'd been told be-bloody-fore to check before he sat down & started. Liam was fed up telling him—the rest of them 'n' all: he was sick to the back teeth of having to drop everything & run & get it for them. They were big enough to know now, all big enough to check afore they started.

'SOME'DY BRING ME UP THE TOILET ROLL!'

Weeboy was getting desperate. Served the wee shite right.

Their mother came in. 'Liam, gaun—for the love of God—take that one up a toilet roll, will ye?'

'I'm fed up taking them up to him, Mum,' he tried to plead. 'He's been told before—'

'I know,' she interrupted, 'but do us a favour 'n' take him one up, will ye? My head can't take any more of this—'

'SOME'DY,' wee bugger was banging the floor now, 'BRING ME UP,' his two shoes off the floor now, 'THE TOI-LET RR-ROOLLLL!!!'

Liam looked at his mother as if he was goney kill the bugger.

'Naw, Liam,' she said. 'Just take him one up.'

She saw him hesitate. 'Gaun,' she said.

He made to go. Was lik he'd no option. Lik he couldn't no do it for her.

'And don't be touching him now!' she warned as he went out the door. 'I don't want you laying a finger on him!'

Liam stopped & looked at her as if he would.

'I'll be in the kitchen when you come back down,' she said. 'An'
I've something to tell you. A favour to ask.'

He looked at her as if to say *What?*

She shook her head but. 'Naw—tell ye when ye get down.'

Cahal was still bawling & hammering as he got him a bog roll from
under the stairs.

'AYE AW RIGHT—I'M COMIN. HOLD YIR HORSES, WILL
YE?'

He'd to open a new pack—to fight with the cellophane—ended
up tearing the tissue while he was at it. It didn't matter, he told himself: would tear where it was going anyhow.

He climbed the stairs, two at a time.

'Here,' he said when he reached the toilet, determined to sound
not-pleased.

The door opened the tiniest wee bit & a hand fished hopefully
for the toilet paper. Liam let him claw fresh air for a bit, then shoved
it into his paw.

'Thanks,' Cahal mumbled.

'Thanks nothing! You're just lucky Mum wants to talk to me!'

The wee bit of trousers down at Cahal's ankles disappeared. The
door closed & the snib rattled shut.

Liam thought of shouting something else, lik he was lucky
it wasn't torn-up bits of the *Paisley Daily Express* he was getting,
thought the better of it but. He was too curious to know what his
mum had to confide in him this time.

He completed the descent in two leaps.

The first took him to the first landing—to the foot-and-a-half
between the bottom step & the landing window. He made sure to
land cleanly.

5.8   5.9   5.8   5.8   5.9   5.4

Bloody Russian judges again! He could just imagine Carpenter or

Coleman having a go at them. Was too professional to let it bother him but. He psyched himself up for the second flight instead. This one was steeper—more stairs anyway.

He made it!

Didn't crash forward onto the holy water font lik the first time he'd tried.

Straight sixes, the judges gave him—'part from the Russians.

The crowd rose to its feet, ecstatic.

He went through to his mum. Didn't say nothing at first, just looked at her expectantly just.

To begin with, she didn't say nothing either. Only handed him a mug of tea she'd poured him, having just made one herself.

'Don't know if your daddy's said anything to ye,' she said, 'but your granda's thinking o' coming over but.'

She meant Granda Cluskey—*her* father. Granda Donnell was dead.

'That's great!' he said, between sips, wishing she'd put less milk in.

'Aye,' she said. 'I'm looking forward to seeing him.'

There was something about the silence that followed.

'How long's he coming for?' Liam asked, concerned.

'Depends. A week. Ten days. Who knows?'

Depends wasn't an answer. He could guess what it depended on but: his da & his granda didn't get on. Well known, it was. Liam hoped to God he was wrong but. For his mum's sake, he hoped he was wrong.

'Do the rest of them know yet?'

He asked to break the silence, more than anything.

'Naw—I thought I'd tell you first. Since you're the oldest, old enough to mind him. The only one old enough to know him properly.'

Liam could feel himself feeling pleased, tried not to let it show but.

His mum was looking kinda sad still. As if she was worried about something. It was lik she was already asking him something before she opened her mouth even.

'What is it,' he risked asking, 'you want me to do?'

'Look after him,' she said, lik it was a relief. 'Look after your granda while he's here. You'll do that for me, love, won't you?'

'Of course,' Liam said, though he couldn't see what the problem was. He'd do it for her lik he did the other things he did. Anything to stop her worrying.

'It's just, wi me back at work 'n' all,' she said. 'He'll be here when you're off studying for your O-Grades. Is that alright, son?'

'Course it is!' he said. He was already looking forward to it. To showing his granda Scotland.

'Thanks, son,' she said & came over & squeezed him. 'I was hoping I could count on you.'

'Is it okay to tell the wee ones?' he asked.

'Course,' she said. 'I just wanted a word wi you first.'

He raced out the back. Couldn't wait to broadcast it. Also the fact Mum'd told *him*.

The day before his granda was due, his mum took him aside again.

He was trying to learn his *Macbeth* quotes—trying & not succeeding—when she found him up in the bedroom.

She'd been next door. 'That was your granda on the phone,' she said.

'What was he saying?'

'The usual,' she said. It looked lik something was worrying her but. 'He's looking forward to coming, looking forward to seeing yous all.'

'Good,' he said. 'But what's wrong? Something's botherin you—'

'He's taken it into his head he wants to go to Carfin,' she said. She looked lik she was goney cry. 'And it's not as if I can take him.'

Liam went over & hugged her. Fact he hadn't a clue where it was, or what it was, didn't come into it. Main thing was to calm Mum down.

'*I'll* take him!' he said. 'Can't be that far away. Why's he wanting to go, anyway?'

'It's a holy place,' she said. 'Somewhere outside Glasgow. They say it's lik Lourdes. Or Fatima. Cept it's over here in Scotland.'

'Never heard of it!' Liam said. He hadn't heard of the Barras or Paddy's Market either, right enough, before Granny Donnell came over. It was funny what themmins over there had heard of sometimes—and you were the ones *living* in the country.

'Is it linked wi the Virgin Mary or what?'

'Think so. That's why he's wanting to go. You know what he's lik wi the Blessed Virgin. D'ye think you could take him?'

'Aye. I'll find out, sure. Wherever it is, there'll be a train or a bus to it. I'll take him when I'm off some day.'

'Thanks, son. That's a weight off my mind so it is. I know I couldn't ask your daddy.'

His granda arrived the next day. Their da picked him up from the airport on the way back from his work. Ciara, it was, said she'd heard him making out he wouldn't've done it otherwise. That oul Pat was just lucky he arrived when he did cos he wouldn't've been giving up his night out at the Hibs to go for him.

Liam made a point of getting his studying done so as he could sit & talk to him. Revision was going well. That was the irregular verbs done for French & all the Third Year stuff for History now. The Liberals 1906–1914 & The Irish Question could wait. There wasn't any rush.

His da pulled up outside & Liam saw the two men get out. His granda had his mac on even though it was lovely. He was waving his big umbrella, pointing at something, as their da lifted his case out.

Liam could've opened the door for them. He watched from the window instead but, let his mum go first.

His da looked lik he was on his best behaviour for once.

'Hello, Daddy!! It's good to see you!'

Mum & Granda were in the hall now. Liam could imagine her kissing him. Granda hugging her back. His da just watching, unimpressed.

'Good to see you, too, love!'

Granda sounded choked. Whatever different ones said when they slagged him off, he sounded choked. Ye had to remember but: he was their mum's dad. Whatever had happened, whatever'd been said, nothing could alter that.

'Come away on in, Daddy. I've made you something to eat—'

Liam got himself ready.

'Hello, Granda!' he said when he seen him—when the big ruddy cheeks came round the door, their da looking serious behind him.

Youngfella didn't know whether to shake hands, or hug him, or nothing at all. In the end-up, he chose nothing at all. Was his granda came over to him.

'Put it there, mucker!' he said, holding his hand out. 'Are ye rightly?'

'Aye,' Liam said as they shook. 'Yourself?'

'Can't complain. Can't complain at all, sure,' his granda said.

Their da rolled his eyes.

'Where's the rest of my grandweans then?'

He was leaning on his big umbrella, Granda, lik he'd stopped to talk in the street.

'At school. Won't be long til they're back now, though.'

'And are you not?'

'I'm on study leave.'

'Study leave, by God!'

'He's got his O-Grades coming up, Daddy, so they stop teaching them. And allow them to study at home—'

'Not that this boy needs to study,' his da said, proudly.

'No half!' Liam said, to disagree. 'I'm no taking anything for granted,' he added when he saw the dirty look he was getting.

It was true. An' anyway, there were times he was scared stiff. Of what could come up in History & Economics. The interpretation in English was a nightmare 'n' all. *Legerdemain* etc. Was always the hard words they asked you what they meant.

'Eight A's he's going for,' his da announced.

'Aye, wi God's holy help,' his mum added.

'That's right, youngfella—you show them! You show them the Irish isn't stupid!' his granda said, poking at the pile of the carpet lik he was poking at chewing gum or something.

'Anyway, he'll be company for you, Daddy, when you're in by yourself,' his mum said.

'Oh don't you be worrying about that,' his granda said. 'I told you on the phone, sure: I'll have my prayers to say. As long as I've a Mass to go to, and peace 'n' quiet to say my prayers, that'll be me contented.'

That night, after the dinner, they sat listening to him. No one could get a word in edgeways. He'd ask you a question & you'd start to answer. Before you got to your point but even, he'd interrupt you— 'Not that I'm interrupting you or anything'—& talk about himself or someone he knew in Derry. Their da gave up after half an hour & went upstairs. He'd stuff to do for the morning, he said— lying, no doubt. Liam noticed even his mum looked put-out but. She didn't lik being interrupted—'Not that I'm interrupting you or anything'—when she was trying to answer a question her father had asked in the first place.

The younger ones didn't seem to notice. The wee ones sat beaming at him just, listening to him, curious. Only wee Orla went all shy, wouldn't go near him. She was definitely going nowhere near him when he showed them his party-trick. When he proved he could wriggle his ear.

It was funny the way he told a story. If the point was who he'd met or what had happened at three in the afternoon, say, he'd start off by telling you about getting up, having a bite of breakfast, brushing his teeth & getting ready for Mass, ten Mass, then maybe talking to this one & that one in the chapel grounds afterwards, listening to their news, their bars, minding you about who they were related to, then he'd maybe popped in to buy a paper on his way from the Cathedral down the town, & he would name all the streets on the way, his accent making Derry sound wild-wild Derry, and, of course, he'd run into this one on Gt. James's St. & that one on William St., & he'd tell you what they'd told him, & it was lik he knew half of Derry & half of Derry knew him, what between the Cathedral & the Bingo on Tuesday & Friday nights, & eventually he'd get to the point where he'd lose his thread & say 'What was I going to tell ye? Oh aye—' & he was off again & the story itself would take two minutes whereas the build-up took half an hour, nearly.

During the stories, sometimes, he'd take his pipe apart & take out his pipe cleaners to clean it. Was a shame the way the white of the cleaners went all stained, Liam thought. Once the pipe was clean & Granda'd looked up it to check, he'd take out his tobacco & fill it, putting some in & pressing it down before he tried to light it. Once it was lit, you'd see him inhaling & watching to see was it lighting right before finally concentrating on his next story.

Sometimes, he wouldn't stop talking to do it & it would be lik he was trying to talk & inhale & exhale & keep an eye on the flame, all at the same time. Other times he'd make wee figures out of the pipe cleaners to entertain the wee ones, before putting them away again.

'Do it again, Granda!' Cahal would laugh. 'Do it again! Please!'

It turned out he'd been in America recently & he told them things about that too. He might as well've stayed in Derry, you'd've thought, to listen to him. Only difference was he walked down 42nd Street to get to 43rd; then gone past 7th Avenue to get to 8th. The Bonars had invited him over. All expenses paid. Wouldn't let him put his hand in his pocket, so they wouldn't. All he had to do was join them.

'That was very good of them!' their mum said.

His granda carried on talking. It was all people Liam didn't know. He wondered whether his mother even knew them. The ones his granda had visited, anyway, were all connected onto the ones in

Newry and Strabane that used to visit Mammy Cluskey's before she died. The ones wi money, in other words. The ones wi the hotel. The hotel their mother and father had taken a coat hanger from, the night Dana won Eurovision. STOLEN FROM CLIFF LAWN HOTEL, it said on it. The whole family had laughed at the meanness of it. Still upstairs in one of the wardrobes, the bloody thing was.

Before the wee ones went to bed, their granda took a comb and paper out & played it lik a mouth organ. Then he started lilting & got their mum to dance. He commented on how good she still was—even after all the weans she'd had. Some of the wee ones looked amazed. They didn't know she'd been a dancer when she was younger.

Soon, the grown-ups were ready for their beds 'n' all. Their granda was obviously tired after the journey & the big long stories were drying up. 'Aye, the travelling will've taken it out of you more than you think, Daddy!' their mum said.

Just as he said he was going up, he finally mentioned their granny. How he'd been in the years since she died. Eight, it would be in the summer, God rest her, he said & he still wasn't over it.

'It's worse than losing your mother or father,' he told their mum. 'You'll see yourself, Bridget, some day, maybe, if Big Liam goes first—not that I'd wish it on either of you. You'll see for yourself then but: losing your partner's worse.'

Their da came back in as Granda was saying that last bit. He didn't say nothing—looked at their mum just. Liam wondered if he *would* say something, thinking back to all his da had said, the summer before in Derry.

Thinking back to what his da had told him, Liam wondered was his mum over Mammy Cluskey dying? Whether you ever got over your mum dying? Ye could live to ninety, he could imagine, & still not be over it. Your mum, after all, was your mum, sure.

The way it worked out, Liam was upstairs & in bed before his granda came up. He got off him & into bed quick. He didn't have pyjamas

& didn't want his granda seeing him.

The only light in the room was the streetlight. It was enough to see by but. Liam'd been looking at wallpaper, studying the German football crest—an eagle, wi DEUTSCHER FUSSBALLBUND round it—when his granda finally came in. His granda didn't turn the light on. Seemed to be looking over to him but.

'You in your bed already?'

'Aye.'

'Speedy Gonzales, eh?'

Liam pretended to laugh.

'Did ye say your bedtime prayers?'

'I'm lying here saying them,' he lied.

It wasn't supposed to. The lie shut Granda up but.

'I'll leave ye to get on wi it then, youngfella,' he said.

The feeling of respect he was giving him was amazing.

Liam now'd to pretend to be praying, he was watching his granda potter round Sean's bed but. It was lik he was working out where things were—how he would do things, where he would put them. Over his shoulders, Liam could still see scenes from the World Cup, lit by the light from the street.

After a minute or so, his granda sat down to take off him & he sat on the bed taking off him. The pyjamas he'd taken out of his case were ready on the bed beside him. A recent *Daily Record* had said that one in every three sleep naked. Everyone Liam knew had pyjamas or slept in their underpants just, just lik him & his da but. He couldn't for the life of him think why anyone would want to be naked.

His granda got changed, starting wi the top half first. Each item got folded & placed on the chair: his pullover, his shirt, his tie. He started to take his vest off, then thought better of it—opened his pyjama top & slipped that on instead. He leant forward to untie his shoes & you heard each shoe, each sock, coming off. The socks went back in the shoes he slid under the chair.

He stood up to take his trousers off. Liam heard the belt being undone, the zip coming down. His granda let the trousers fall, then stepped out of them, taking a moment to line up the creases. Only once he was satisfied, did he place them over the chair. He looked funny, in his pyjama top just & thermal underwear. Lik something you'd see on the telly. *On Ilka Moor bah't 'at* 'n' all that, *On Il-ka Moor—bah't—'at.*

His granda sat down on the bed again, lifted & unfolded his pyjama trousers. He tugged a bit at the cords. Just as it looked lik he'd pull them on, he raised his bum & slipped his long johns off. His big bare bum shone in the streetlight. It wasn't that Liam had seen many bums—this had to be the whitest ever but. He seen it again when his granda stood up to get into his trousers properly. Lik a big round ball of chalk, it was, if big balls of chalk even existed, that is. Liam looked away. Concentrated on letting on to pray.

His granda adjusted the cords, tied them, & got down on his knees. He was facing Liam's bed now—making it harder to keep pretending. Liam could see the prayer book, totally bulging wi prayer cards. The rosary beads were out in front of him 'n' all. This, Liam could tell, could take a while. All night, if he was unlucky.

He wondered how he was goney survive. A bright idea saved him.

'Father, Son, Holy Ghost, Amen,' he muttered, loud enough for his granda to hear, & blessed himself. 'That's me done. Night, night, Granda!' he said & turned to face the wall.

'Night, night,' his granda said. 'I'll not be long, son. I just want to say a decade or two.'

He *was* long. An' the worst thing was, Liam'd to lie there listening, even though there wasn't a sound, 'cept maybe for his granda's knees cracking, or him removing or replacing a prayer card. Liam'd forgot but he minded now but: one time in Derry hearing about his granda falling off of the scaffolding when he was working over in England. His cartilages had to be removed.

The rosary beads were going now and, to begin wi, Liam lay try-ing to guess which decade his granda was at. How many Hail Mary's he'd said. How many were still to go before the next Glory Be. It was a bit lik turning the sound down on your favourite record & keep-ing singing it in your head—then turning the sound back up to see if you'd kept up. Soon, he was trying to guess whereabouts in the Hail Mary his granda was—first half or second? Or *Now and at the hour of our death. Amen.*

He hoped to God his granda wasn't goney kneel there—just across from him—praying for a happy death. He could only half remember, minded having to say the Prayer for a Happy Death but as a weeboy in Derry. Whenever they said the Rosary.

Jesus, Mary and Joseph, I give you my heart and my soul.

Jesus, Mary and Joseph, something, something, something.

Then:

Jesus, Mary and Joseph, assist me at my last agony.

That last bit had scared the shit out of him as a weeboy even. He wasn't looking forward to that, he wasn't: his last agony.

It was spooky. Definitely spooky: lying this close to someone talking to God. Strange thing was: every Sunday at Mass, the whole congregation talked to God supposedly, & it didn't bother him a bit. He also heard the wee ones saying their prayers every night & that didn't bother him either. This but was different. Was lik something out of Dickens. Or lik Fr. Fallon & the totally unnatural way he said *This is my body* & *This is my blood* every Sunday. Aye, that was it—it was the intensity that scared him: the darkness, the silence, his gran-da, the age he was. A dying age, surely to God? More than anything else but, it was the thought of his granda's special intentions. It was lik he was eaves-bloody-dropping on his granda's special intentions, for God's sake—though he couldn't hear a word. He remembered the comment about losing a partner & wondered what his granda asked God for, for Mammy Cluskey.

It was spooky as hell alright: his granda & God deep in conver-sation in his & Sean's bedroom—& him himself lying in the dark, across in the other bed. Liam lay there dreading it: dreading one of them—God or his granda—interrupting themselves to concentrate on him. What if God told his granda something bad? About that wee scoundrel over at the window?

He must've fallen asleep, Liam. He must've fallen asleep & now he was wide awake again. He was on the verge of throwing his pillow at Sean when he realised it was his granda snoring. He looked across. The old man looked that peaceful. So much so he could be dead. It was okay but—the blankets were going up & down & up & down. His cheeks even looked lik they were smiling even.

Liam tried, it was no use but: he couldn't get back to sleep. Even lying there was even hurting. He threw back the blankets & sat against the wall, taking care not to catch the windowsill. Would be a sore one if his head done that.

The wall turned out to be cold & the wood-chip was annoying his back so he slipped the pillow behind him. He pulled his knees up & hugged them, rested his chin between them. The whole time he sat lik this, his eyes remained fixed on his granda. Was lik he was staring at him, trying to work something out.

His other gran, those rare times she phoned, would mention seeing his granda in town sometimes. The Star Bingo was where often she seen him. 'Still a fine-lookin man!' she'd insist—then tease them about other *weemin*. She'd seen him walking with a woman down the Strand, she'd claim. He was a real gentleman too, she'd insist, rubbing it in. He always walked on the outside, sure. Allowed the lady to walk on the inside. Aye, their Granda Cluskey knew how to treat a lady, alright.

He was in no hurry to go to Heaven, to be wi Mammy Cluskey again, it sounded lik, when Mammy Donnell told stories lik that.

Liam lay down again. Lay there just, twisting 'n' turning but. Completely & totally confused, he was. He didn't know what to think. Was everything his da said true? Should he hate his granda lik his da did? Not lik him & trust him lik he used to, at least? Part of him wanted to lik his granda still—for his mum's sake. For his Mammy Cluskey in Heaven's sake too. Whatever he'd done or not done, he was still his granda, sure. An' however much Granda'd hurt her, or not hurt her, their mum was always goney feel a daughter's love for him. That was the bottom line. Even their da saw that, admitted that. Was him that said it to Liam, sure.

It was no use: he couldn't get back to sleep. There was no way he could slip downstairs either & have a drink, say. He'd have to walk round the bed, then open the door, sure, & he was afraid of wakening Granda.

He sat up again. The more he sat looking at Granda, the more he thought about what their da had said in Derry that night. He'd thought about it before & he'd think about it again. It was the night, after all, he'd had to grow up. The night he'd stopped being a boy.

He'd ended up breaking down in tears. He could nearly cry again now, thinking about it. He'd been sitting in Mammy Donnell's house, at the end of the sofa nearest the door, his da in the armchair nearest the telly, & he'd broken down in tears in the middle of it.

'What's wrong?' his da'd asked.

'It's Mum. I feel sorry for Mum,' he'd answered.

It was true; it was also lyin through his teeth but. He was above all sad himself.

It was lik everything his da'd told him that night had taken something away. It was lik Mammy Cluskey dying again. 'Cept worse than that.

He'd cried & cried, still not admitting what was really wrong. He'd just stayed sitting where he was & his da'd stayed sitting where he was & any time his da asked what was wrong, he claimed it was Mum—he felt sorry, sad, for Mum.

'Will you promise me something?' his da asked when he stopped breaking his heart.

Liam nodded.

'Always look after your mum,' his da said. 'Whatever happens, always look after your mum. Will ye promise me that?'

Liam gulped & nodded.

'You don't need to worry about me. I can look after myself. Always always but, make sure your Mum's okay.'

'I do the same for my mother,' he added.

Liam bit his lip, to make sure the crying'd stopped.

'You promise?'

'Promise,' he nodded.

Two saracens drove past the window. His da couldn't see them from where he was, but Liam did but. It was alright, though: there wouldn't be no stone-throwing. Not at this hour of night.

As if the Troubles weren't bad enough, the family in Derry—the McCluskeys, at least—was at war, divided down the middle. That's what Liam learned that night. Years after the funeral, the family was still divided. The two wee ones against the three big ones, it was. And his mother had been allocated a camp, whether she liked it or not. Whether she liked it or not, his da explained, that was how the rest of them saw it.

It was all over what had happened to the house. The house & buckin garage. 'They're lucky to have that problem,' his Mammy Donnell had said, his da told him. 'If they rented from the Corporation lik I do, they wouldn't have that problem.' 'She has a point, of course,' his da said.

His mum, being his mum, had tried to heal the rift, his da continued. 'I wouldn't've,' he commented. 'And your aunt Senga—ye want to hear her on the subject—wouldn't've tried either. Nor would your uncle Carl have—and he's your Granda's son. Paddy and Fiona agree wi us 'n' all, but they're in Gibraltar now. Your mum, being your mum, did try—and only succeeded in getting hurt again. They're a shower, son. A buckin shower. Best of it is: your mother brought them all up, ye know. No life of her own she had, bringing them all up. Your granda had your granny out working, to pay for the house, so your mother'd to bring the younger ones up. An' that's the thanks she gets. All the buckin thanks she gets. From oul Pat himself—and from her brother 'n' buckin sister. That's gratitude for you, son.'

It hurt, listening. It made him grow up but. After that, after listening to his da that night, there was no way he could be a wee-boy any more. He'd to forget everything he used to think. It was all wrong. People weren't, things weren't, the way he thought they were.

The next few days passed without fuss. His granda got up & went to ten Mass & would stay on in the chapel to pray. By the time he came down the road, Liam would have his revision done & would've started to make lunch. His granda smiled as he watched him.

'You're right 'n' handy in the kitchen, son. It's good to see you can do it. I had to learn it after your granny, God rest her, died.'

Liam didn't know what he was on about. It wasn't much he could do—but he could open a tin of hamburgers, at least. Or put together a salad. Or make a wicked cheese & toast.

Sometimes his granda got him to tell him what he'd been learn-ing while he made the things or while the two of them ate & Liam would rhyme off the History he'd been revising. He was still wor-ried about History & Economics the most. Or he'd explain the Law of Diminishing Returns—the shape of the curve—how it rose & then fell & then collapsed. The pleasure you got from the first ba-nana. The maybe even better second banana. The amazing third. Then but, the not-so-nice fourth banana. An' so on & so on, until the make-you-puke seventeenth. His granda would laugh at that bit. Say he couldn't see what he was worried about. 'You talk a fine game, anyway, son. If you can write it down half as well as you ex-plain it to me, you'll have nothing to worry about!'

After lunch, it was time to sit down to his Languages. He always looked forward to that bit. It didn't feel lik work at all. The only thing about Languages was: they were hard to talk about. At most, ye could let people hear some. Not that he knew what to say, ever, when someone wanted to hear some. *Say something in German* or *Say something in French for me*. You never knew what the hell to say when they suddenly hit you wi that.

He taught his granda *Geschwindigkeitsbeschränkungen*. The German for *speed limits*, it was, & part of his own first lesson. His granda had laughed when he told him, was rhyming it off in no time. Thought it was great, he did. 'Best of it is: people'll think I can say a whole bloody sentence,' he joked, 'when I tell them that one!'

The time just flew by when they were together. Each day, it seemed lik no time at all before the rest of the weans were home from school & his mum was home from work.

'Did that boy behave himself for you, Daddy?' his mum pretended to ask.

'You don't even have to ask,' his granda would answer. 'The youngfella's a credit to ye. He's no bother at all. Your mother, God rest her soul, would be proud if she could see him.'

On the Thursday, they went to Carfin. Their da came home & told them what Liam'd already found out. Bus to Paisley first, of course. From the stop at the bottom of the Steps. They then needed a train to Glasgow. Then one to Motherwell. They'd be better off taking a bus for the last bit—to Carfin itself—but.

'The Blessed Virgin hadn't all that bother, I bet ye!' his da joked.

They were a bit late setting off as his granda insisted on attending ten Mass. 'I can save my prayers for Carfin,' he said, 'but I'd still rather go to Mass, than not.'

It was great, getting the trains. Liam could still count on one hand the number of times he'd been on one. The first time'd been with his granny to Portrush. He could still mind a lady opening a Bounty up, the two bars on cardboard inside the wrapping. It had looked that nice & she'd offered him a piece. The coconut had made him sick but.

Not long after Mammy Cluskey died, Granda Cluskey took him, too. 'Thon was the first time he went anywhere after your granny died,' his mum explained to him long after they'd emigrated. 'He asked if he could take you with him so I had to say aye, of course. I had to let him.'

'It was the best thing we could've done,' she added, after thinking a bit. 'Having you with him brought him out of himself.'

Liam could remember the trip well—but hadn't realised the significance of it but. He just minded buying the wee brass candlesticks as a present for his mum. He'd spotted them as it was time to take the train home & wanted to buy her them. Turned out he'd only the money for one, but his granda'd given him the money for the other one so as he could buy them both. Liam'd told his mum, years later in Scotland. 'So one was really from Granda,' he'd admitted. She'd smiled. 'Doesn't matter,' she'd said, 'Doesn't matter one bit. I'll always treasure them.'

'Thon was the first present you ever bought me, any of yous ever bought me,' she'd explained.

That had got Liam thinking again: 'bout how, when you done them or said them, you didn't realise the significance of things always. Sometimes they meant more to other people than you yourself realised.

The train that took them to Motherwell was on its way to London.

His granda'd been there 'n' all. 'It's some place,' he said. 'By God, it's some place. Go there some time when you grow up and you'll see for yourself. It's no place to live in. By God, it isn't. You'll never tire of visiting the place but.'

He rhymed off names Liam knew from the telly: Picadilly, Euston, Leicester Square, the Thames. It was funny hearing London place-names in a Derry accent.

His granda suggested lunch before the bus to Carfin.

'We wouldn't want to leave it any later,' he said.

They went to a place called WIMPEY. *We Import More Pakis Every Year* was what it stood for, people said. The 'P' but could've stood for *Paddies* too.

There was a WIMPEY next to Central in Glasgow, but Liam'd never been in it. When he saw the prices, he wanted to head back out.

'See the price of that beef burger?' he asked his granda, pointing to it.

His granda looked, wondering what was wrong.

'I could make you four for that price!' he said. 'The tin I opened for lunch the other day cost less than they're asking here for one!'

They ordered anyway. His granda said just to go ahead, even though Liam said he'd choke on it, what wi the prices they were asking.

His granda had to laugh. He even told the waitress who took their order. The woman laughed too. 'It's not me sets the prices, son,' she said. 'They're very popular, anyway, despite the price.'

As they waited for the beef burgers, Liam kept remembering what he'd been taught in Economics. He told his granda what the teacher'd said about chains. One price would be set for across the country. Each and every branch would be the same. London would be identical to Motherwell. That way, you got economies of scale. 'Not that they're passing them on to the consumer!' he said as the woman approached wi their dinners.

His granda and the woman looked at him just—then laughed.

Liam couldn't think what your woman had to laugh about but. An invisible cost was what she was.

'Time's getting on!' his granda said when they were nearly done. 'Carfin next! I wouldn't mind a wee look at Wishaw as well on the way back. I was over here working after the war, you see, son, and wouldn't mind seeing what it looks lik now. Don't worry, it isn't far.'

Rush or no rush, Granda insisted on brushing his teeth. He never ate without doing them again, he said, leaving Liam to go to the toilet.

His teeth were all pipe-stained—all tanny-brown at the bottom—nevertheless. Moss on gravestones was what it was lik.

They left the WIMPEY and jumped on a bus. CARFIN, it said on the front. His granda still insisted on asking did it go there but. 'Does it go past the grotto?' he asked. The driver nodded. 'Could you maybe give us a shout when we get to the nearest stop?' The driver said he would. They made such a fuss, half the bloody bus would.

It was only a mile or so, somebody told them. A bit of stopping & starting in the centre of Motherwell itself made it seem longer but. Eventually they were heading along a big long road out of town, wi houses, some big, on either side. The road went down & down & down before it went up & up again. It made Liam feel nervous. It felt lik: now, if they were lost, they'd be lost-lost.

The place they entered looked lik something out of the Wild West.

'At's the grotty comin up noo, mister!' someone called out.

Sure enough, the driver turned round. 'That's Carfin Grotto now, sir,' he said, as if he'd forgot.

'Thank you kindly. Thank you kindly,' Granda said, getting off.

It was hard to see what the fuss was all about. One minute you were at the entrance, the next you were in the grounds, the next you were at the grotto itself. Okay, ye could see some work had gone into the place, the gardens 'n' that—the whole place looked as grey as the weather but. If this was what Lourdes or Fatima looked lik, God alone knew why people travelled there.

They went straight up to the grotto & stood at it.

BEHOLD
THY
MOTHER

it said in metal lettering above the Virgin Mary—though the leaves blotted most of the THY out.

'She doesn't look anything lik my mother!' Liam thought. He nearly joked to his granda. Didn't but, in case he offended him.

I AM THE IMMACULATE CONCEPTION

it said, also in metal lettering, above what looked lik annexes, higher up & further along. There was other writing too, not all in capitals but, that needed a lick of paint. There was something a bit shabby about all the metalwork. 'A fresh coat of paint wouldn't go amiss,' his granda said, looking at it. 'Wouldn't it not?'

Before they started praying, his granda told him what he knew about the shrine. No, the Blessed Virgin hadn't appeared here— it was Polish workers, ordinary men with a great devotion to the Virgin Mary, who'd built it. He didn't say—didn't know—how the Poles came to be in Scotland. Why they'd built it here & not in Poland. 'Thanksgiving, it will've been, son. An act of thanksgiving. I don't know what for but, right enough,' he added. 'Something to do wi the war maybe.'

His granda took his rosary beads out. It was time to start praying.

'You could say a wee prayer and ask to do well in your O-Levels,' his granda suggested.

Liam nodded though he knew he wouldn't. Knew not to ask for anything for himself. Not since he was a wean & had prayed in vain for a watch. 'Just cos you want it, doesn't mean you're goney get it!' his da had said. God seemed to be the same.

Naw, at most, he'd ask that when the results came out in August, he wouldn't let his mum & dad down. They'd be over in Derry when the time came, he knew, & they'd have to be posted over. He could already imagine the postman coming down Gran's path & him taking them & hiding in the toilet to open them & reading them line by line as they came out of the envelope. He'd pray to God he wouldn't disappoint them. Specially wi them being in Derry, he didn't want to let them down—his mum, especially.

Needless to say, his granda was still going strong & looking totally holy-holy when Liam'd finished his own prayers. He'd even said a prayer for his French teacher's mother and German teacher's father who'd died before Xmas. Still didn't come close to matching his granda but.

Couple of songs came into his head as he waited: the "Love to Love" one he'd heard the tail end of at breakfast & "Kisses for Me" (the Eurovision entry). He nearly did the wee dance, just to warm up.

His granda must've seen he wasn't concentrating.

'Say a wee prayer for your Granny in Heaven, son,' he asked gently, sadly.

'I already have,' Liam answered.

They looked at each other & a look crossed his granda's face. He even stopped praying to hug him.

'She'd be proud of ye, son. She'd be truly proud of you.'

Liam gulped. Was lik something did a reverse in his throat.

There was no doubt about it: he loved that woman to bits still.

'Let's have a wee dander round the grounds before that wind gets any worse!' his granda said when he was finished.

Wind or no wind, Liam was glad of the walk. Getting moving warmed him up, at least. Not that the statues did anything for him. Statues never did.

They didn't explore everything. Hardly bothered wi up the back. From where they stopped, sure, they could see a big ugly factory through the trees. They could hear it 'n' all.

It was lik the aftermath of a chess match, Liam decided, looking round. There was no board, of course—just green lawns. It looked lik White had just decimated Black. Wherever you looked, only white marble pieces remained. The white but, for Liam, was too white but.

On the way out, his granda stopped briefly at the Little Flower. His holy-holy look was fading already, Liam noticed—the cold wind, the dander round, must've done it.

'Time to go!' his granda announced suddenly. 'That wind would cut through you, sure.'

As they left the grounds, a bus for Wishaw was whizzing towards their bus stop. They'd never make it, Liam thought. His granda, but, waved it down. You'd've thought he thought he was somebody, way he did it wi his brolly. The driver—a different one this time—seemed impressed anyway. Couldn't have been more polite. His granda's satisfaction, certainly, was there for all to see—his big ruddy grin filling the deck.

Liam concentrated on looking out the window.

There was something about the place made you realise round here *could* be nice. You got the odd hint of the hills & countryside surrounding it. An' it wasn't as if there was any shortage of trees. Was just a shame about all the ugly stuff bang in front of you: the run-down council houses, the tower blocks, the scrap-yards, the rough-looking bars. The heavy industry, of course. The chimneys & the smoke pouring out of them.

There was something *hard* about the folk you saw 'n' all. The women especially. No way would he go wi a weegirl from these parts.

They ended up not actually entering Wishaw. A couple of stops before—Liam'd just spotted a "Town Centre: 1/2 mile" sign—his granda jumped up suddenly & asked could they get off. He'd recognised something. Recognised something from before. This was the place he'd been. It was round here somewhere he'd worked. Round here somewhere the Boyles had lived.

They set off walking back down the hill again. One minute his granda was sure they were right, the next he had his doubts. 'I think I remember them there houses,' he said, pointing to older-style red sandstone ones, on their right. 'But I don't remember them there.' The group on the left had "1963" on the gable, Liam spotted. 'Aye, you're right, mucker,' his granda said when he pointed it out. 'I should bear in mind it's been thirty years nearly. It's bound to have changed some in that time.'

They came to a row of shops which were all new now. His granda was convinced he recognised them though.

'That there was the barber's,' he said. 'And there was an Italian next door. Sold lovely sweets and chocolate, the boy did.' You could see how good they'd been, to look at him. 'And the one at the end was a paper shop.'

They carried on walking. Houses were missing from the other side of the road, if his granda wasn't mistaken. Liam hoped he wasn't—his shoes were now hurting & his patience running out. He wouldn't've minded if his granda was seeing what he wanted to. The thought of them running round in circles but, without finding anything, was starting to do his head in.

'Did you lik living here?' he asked, for the sake of it just.

His granda snorted, sort of. 'It was an Orange hole, to be honest, son. But I met some lovely people. Aye, some of the people were alright—lik anywhere else you go!'

He told him about his digs—his landlady & how strict she was. The different boys he'd worked wi.

All of a sudden, he came to a halt. They'd got to the point where nothing at all looked familiar. Where he recognised sweet-fanny-adams.

'Except, maybe, that street of houses. That rings bells,' he said.

He stood there, trying to fathom it. That's what he always said: he tried to *fathom* things. Sometimes he couldn't, no matter how he tried—couldn't fathom whatever it was out.

It was now definitely starting to seem pointless & Liam was beginning to want home. He was thinking of the things he could be doing. Pillans & Wilsons—he could be working on Pillans & Wilsons papers. Even if he hated them, even if they looked lik Mass leaflets, even if they were harder than the actual O-Grades, he could still be doing them for practice.

'I'd love to see the Boyles again,' his granda said. 'It's been a lovely day, but that would be the icing on the cake. I wonder how I could find out where they live. Whether there's any of them around still.'

Three doors along, a woman in a headscarf and raincoat came out. Her dog was on a lead.

'I'll ask this lady!' his granda said.

Fat chance, Liam thought.

'Excuse me, love, I wonder if you could help me?' his granda said as the woman passed.

She stopped, as if frightened by the accent.

'I'm over visiting from Ireland,' his granda explained.

'I'd never've guessed, wi that brogue!' The woman laughed.

His granda laughed too. He told her about being over from Derry nearly thirty years before & knowing a family called Boyle.

'The woman in that house wi the red door was a Boyle,' the woman said. 'She's Mary Robertson now. Boyle was her maiden name but.'

'Mary Boyle,' his granda said. He shook his head. 'Can't say it rings bells. But then, I suppose it was the boys in the family I knew. She could always be a sister. Maybe a younger sister I wouldn't've known.'

'Give it a go, anyway,' the woman said. 'There's no harm in trying. Worst they can do is say no.'

They went up to the red door. Liam couldn't believe they were doing this. As they went up the path & climbed the steps, he was aware of folk looking out. His granda must've been, too.

His granda rang the doorbell.

Liam hid behind him—this could be ultra-embarrassing.

A wee boy wi a turn in his eye opened the door.

'Is your mammy in, son?'

'Aye—MUM!' he roared. 'It's a man—for you!'

He opened the door wide & Liam saw they had carpet. They'd the phone in 'n' all. An' there was a space hopper up against the table it was on. The face on it smiled at them as if to say, 'Yous crazy?'

The boy's mum came out & his granda explained the whole spiel to her. The name Pat McCluskey meant nothing to her but, just lik Mary Boyle had meant nothing to him.

'Do you remember the names of the boys in the family at all?' she asked.

'Well, John was the one I knew best. And I'm sure the other one was Tom.'

'John and Tom Boyle? That could be my cousins John and Thomas. My aunt Teresa and uncle Paul's two boys.'

His granda's face lit up. 'Of course! Paul and Teresa Boyle! How could I forget?! I suppose—to me at the time—they were Mr. and Mrs. Boyle, right enough.'

'They're dead now, of course, God have mercy on them,' the woman said. 'Dead, this long while.' Then: 'Sorry—I'm forgetting my manners—come on in 'n' sit down 'n' I'll make you a cup of tea.'

'I wouldn't lik to impose on you, lik,' his granda said, 'but thanks, I will.'

'Are John and Tom still local?' he asked as he sat down.

'Thomas died last year,' the woman answered.

'Oh—I'm sorry to hear that,' his granda said.

'Aye. Thomas died last year, God love him,' the woman repeated. 'It was very sad. Cancer. The boy was no age either. Same age as my husband.'

'God, that's sad.'

'Aye, it's right what they say: ye never know the day. John's still around though. I'll just put the kettle on, then I'll phone him for you. He's not even ten minutes away, so if he's in, he should be able to pop round.'

She went into the kitchen to put the kettle on.

'Will the boy drink a cup too?'

Liam had to say he didn't drink tea. He'd stopped two days before.

'Coffee?'

'I don't drink coffee either.'

'What do you drink?'

'Nothing.'

It was true—but it felt terrible, wi the woman trying to be kind to him.

'I'll take a drink of orange if you have that,' he said.

'Diluting?'

'That would be lovely, thanks,' he said, lying through his teeth.

His granda nodded up at photos on the mantelpiece.

'That'll be Mary's family,' he said. There were only three of them. 'The oldest boy looks about your age!' his granda said.

Liam agreed. Thought it would be nice to meet him. Boy looked friendly.

The woman returned after a minute or two. 'I got John in,' she said. 'He remembers you fine. He says can you give him ten minutes?'

'Course I can!' his granda said. 'Aw, that's great! Thanks very much, Mary, love. I'm looking forward to seeing him.'

The woman brought in tea & biscuits on a tray. She'd her best china out. Even the diluting orange was in a cup.

Liam took it & sipped at it. He hated the feel of delft. It was always that thin, that fine, against your lips. He hated the patterns 'n' all. To make things worse, Mary had skimped with the orange & the water—she hadn't let it run—was lukewarm.

He took a Bourbon to try & take his mind off it.

'That'll be your own children up there then?' his granda asked, pointing to the photos. 'They look lovely!'

'Aye, that's the three mahoods,' she said. 'Peter, the middle one, opened the door to you. My eldest boy's Christopher, and my wee girl's Helen. She's four.'

'What age is Christopher?'

'Seventeen, coming up. He did his O-Grades last year.'

'Liam here's doing his this year.'

'Is he? Are ye feeling confident?'

Liam shrugged, as if to say okay. Least she didn't say he looked too young. Turning fifteen, he'd be, just as they started.

'Christopher did alright in the end. Better than expected. I'll get him to let you see his certificate when he comes in.'

'That would be great. I've never seen what they look like,' Liam said.

He concentrated on the biscuits as the woman & his granda

chatted. Concentrated on getting the orange down.

'Would you like some more?' the woman asked, standing up, soon as she seen he was finished. 'I've no more biscuits. Could make you toast but.'

'No thanks. That was plenty, thanks,' he said.

'You're very welcome to have more,' she insisted, but still he said no.

He was saved by the front door going.

'Oh—that'll be John now!' she said to his granda. She looked as if she would head to the door, then stopped suddenly & turned to his granda again.

'I should maybe prepare you, Pat,' she said. 'John had a bad stroke last year. One side of his face has been twisted ever since. And he gets very embarrassed about a twitch he's developed—'

'Oh don't you worry about that now, Mary. I'll not let on I notice. Wi the Troubles back home, we're used to that kinda thing. We hardly blink. Naw, don't you be worrying about that now, love!'

She went to let John in.

'Paddy McCluskey!' John just about roared when he saw him. 'God Almighty! Fancy seeing you again!'

'Great to see you, John, son,' his granda said, jumping up to hug him.

It was noticeable that John was a good bit younger.

They pulled back from the hug & studied each other.

John was wearing a suit. Liam wondered whether he'd already been wearing it, or whether he'd pulled it on specially. Didn't go wi the shirt he was wearing, that was for sure.

'I was wild sorry to hear about Thomas dying,' his granda said, as if not to comment on John's face. 'That's sad now—very sad indeed.'

John, still pained, nodded.

'You're still going strong, though, I see!' his granda said, as if to jolt him out of it.

John shook his head sadly. Ye could see he wasn't going to allow Granda to gloss over anything.

'Naw, Pat,' he said. 'I'm not the man I was either. I suffered a very bad stroke last year. Don't tell me you didn't notice my face now!'

His granda, for once, was speechless. Totally stuck for words, he was. Liam watched to see what comment he would make—him that wasn't goney make any.

'You survived it, John. That's the main thing. You're still with us, thanks be to God. Your face could still come round, sure. Give it time & it could still come round.'

'Naw, Pat,' he said. 'This is me to my dyin day. That's the way it is, just. No point in making out it isn't. Naw, I'm stuck wi this bloody twitch.'

It twitched even more, now he mentioned it.

His granda patted him. Tried to comfort him. 'You never know now, John. Never say never now. Wi God's holy help, it might yet go. Go of its own accord. Don't you be fretting yourself now. Worrying about it's the one thing that could make it worse.'

John twitched again. He turned & focused on Liam. Was lik desperation the way he did it—anything, to get away from the twitch.

'Who's this young fella?'

'My grandson. Liam. The eldest. Bridget's eldest.'

John shook hands wi him—'Hello, Liam, son!'—then turned to his granda again.

'How many have you?'

'Twenty, at the last count. There'll be more, no doubt, if God spares me to see them.'

'You and Ita must be very proud.'

'Ita's dead, John, these eight years. I lost her eight years ago—'

John saw what went through him when he said it & took his arm.

'I know how it feels, Pat. I lost my Maureen too, sure. Year and a half ago.'

'And had you a family?'

'Naw, Pat. It didn't seem to be God's will. Naw, Pat. No weans. No grandweans. You count your lucky blessings now,' he said, looking him in the eye, all serious. 'Even if you did lose Ita, you count your lucky blessings.'

His granda nodded, all serious 'n' all.

'I know, John. I do. I thank God every morning and night, I do.'

'Will you have a cup of tea, John?' Mary asked.

He nodded & they both took a seat. Mary gave Liam comics to look at before she headed out. The *Victors* & *Hotspurs* he'd ignore—he could never see the attraction of them. There was a couple of *Roy of the Rovers* stories he'd enjoy but.

Soon, he was engrossed in what he was reading. Every now & again but, he looked up at his granda & John, distracted by them laughing. Yapping away, the two of them were. It was funny seeing his granda wi one of his old pals. Talking about times they'd shared. It seemed to take years off the both of them. John's face had stopped twitching even, more or less.

'Liam,' his granda interrupted him at one point.

He looked up.

'John's just telling me it wasn't the Poles.'

He must've looked puzzled.

'Carfin! It wasn't the Poles. Seems there was a plaque we could've read at the entrance. It was *miners* laid the gardens—'

'Aye, at the time of the General Strike,' John confirmed.

'Aw right,' Liam said.

They'd done 1926 at school, so he knew about it. He hadn't realised it was in Scotland too but. It had just been in England, he'd thought—to listen to the teacher, anyway.

'So it wasn't the Poles, after all,' his granda said. 'I must've confused it wi something else—'

'Aye, it was definitely before the war, Pat,' John said. 'I'm sure o' that. The fiftieth anniversary's this year, sure.'

Liam thought about it. He liked things lik that. The bits in History where folk stood up for themselves. For things they knew were right. Also the fact they were still remembered. Fifty years on, they hadn't been forgotten. He liked that 'n' all.

'Naw, it wasn't just devotion to the Blessed Virgin, Pat,' he heard John insisting. 'It also gave them something to do. And respectability. Folk couldn't condemn them for not working, accuse them of being idle, when they were doing something worthwhile like that, sure!'

His granda was suggesting they should hit the road again when Christopher turned up. They heard the back door opening & he came in through the kitchen. There might only've been a year between them, but Liam thought Christopher looked older—older than in the photograph certainly. He looked more mature—more of a grown man. He was obviously more full of himself, too, as he stood there in his tracksuit, giving as good as he got.

Mary introduced him & Liam.

'You're some size of a youngfella!' his granda said. 'Are ye coortin yet?'

'Is he coortin?' his mother laughed. 'It's lock up your daughters wi that one!'

'Aye, ahm coortin alright!' Christopher confirmed.

'I don't think this boy is!' his granda said, nodding at Liam.

Liam could've cursed him.

'Nothing wrong wi that. Sure there's time. All the time in the world,' Mary said. 'He'll not want for admirers either, to look at him.'

Liam blushed. Mary must've seen it—was lik she changed the subject deliberately.

'Christopher, Liam's doing his O-Grades this year. Goney let him see the certificate you got? Would be nice for him to see what it looks like.'

Christopher disappeared upstairs, came back down with a big brown envelope.

'I've seen the envelope before,' Liam said, taking it. 'We'd to fill one in before Christmas. The teacher told us about all the boys who get their address wrong every year.'

'I suppose some of them wouldn't be wanting to see their results!' John joked. 'I know I wouldn't!'

'Not this boy!' his granda said. 'Eight A's he's going for!'

Liam could've kilt him.

Mary said nothing. Written all over her but, it was.

It was obvious, to look at Christopher, what he was thinking too.

Liam wasted no time in opening the envelope, afraid Christopher could take it back. That's not what happened but. Youngfella just hunkered down beside his mum & started talking again.

The certificate was amazing.

Liam studied it carefully. It was on really nice thick white card & had the crest & two owls at the top of it.

SCOTTISH CERTIFICATE OF EDUCATION

it said beneath the crest, in great big capital letters. The S, C, and E, bigger still. The style of the print made it look really formal—really serious—lik it was worth something.

There was a whole lot of blurb before you got to the results. The *Scottish Certificate of Education Examination Board hereby certified*— Christopher's middle name was Eugene—& he was *presented* by a school Liam had never heard tell of & had *obtained* the following *awards*. Christopher'd only got three. A "C" in Biology. A "D" in English. An' a "D" in Arithmetic. Liam wondered what had happened to the rest. Everyone in his school, sure, did eight.

The others were still busy talking so he turned the certificate over & read the small print. The first note—about erasures or alterations not authorised by the signature of the Director of the Exam Board rendering the certificate *invalid*—put the wind up him even though he'd never do that. The second explained the percentages that went with the grades. There was a comparison with the system before 1973, then a sentence that went right through him: *Performances be-*

low E are not entered on the Certificate. That must be what had happened to Christopher. Liam could hardly take the other notes in—stuff about Engineering Science & Secretarial Studies, mainly—for thinking about it. This must be what the other boys at school called a "no mention." The other thing they talked about—the "Comp O"—he found under the third note. He read & re-read it. Turned out you could only get that—the COMPENSATORY ORDINARY GRADE AWARD—if you'd failed your *Higher*. If you failed your O-Grade, you got buck all.

Bucksake.

Enough to give you nightmares, it was.

When it was clear they were about to leave, Liam handed the certificate back.

'Thanks for letting me see it, Christopher,' he said. He didn't comment on his results.

'Mind now,' his granda was saying as they stepped out into the garden, 'don't you be worrying about that twitch, John. It's not as bad as you make out. So don't be over-sore on yourself. Mind now—cos worrying might only make it worse. Just you try & forget about it—and wi God's holy help, it might go away.'

John shook his head. Was having none of it. As far as he was concerned, it was never goney get better.

'I'm telling you now,' Granda tried to insist still—so much so, it was embarrassing, 'the best thing you could do's forget about it. Just forget about it—and who knows, it could clear up by itself.'

'Nice meeting you all,' Liam said when he got a chance, to bring an end to the proceedings.

'Aye, you too,' Mary replied. 'And mind,' she added for his granda, 'just follow the road up and round & right at the lights & you'll find your bus stop, no bother.'

She let him go wi'out mentioning his O-Grades, Liam noticed, wi'out wishing him luck. She was too *whatever* to wish him luck.

His granda was still on about John's twitch on the bus. He was all for returning to the grotto & praying for a miracle. 'I hope he manages to forget about it,' he was still insisting. 'Besides the power of prayer, thon's the one thing that could take it away—or even alleviate it: managing to forget all about it.'

Liam hoped to God no one on the bus knew which John his granda was talking about, given the rate he was going on about it. He just wouldn't let go of the subject.

By the time they got home, three trains & two buses later, they were dog-tired. They'd had long waits between trains, unlike in the morning. They'd hardly talked as they travelled. It wasn't that they weren't talking but.

His granda ended up looking his age for once.

'Did yous have a nice day?' his mum asked.

'Aye—lovely, love! It fairly took it out of me but,' his granda said. 'I'll tell you all about it tomorrow. I wouldn't mind heading straight up the stairs, to be honest, and getting on wi my prayers. I'm ready for collapsing, to tell the God's truth.'

'Aye, you look it. I can see it to look at ye, Daddy,' his mum said. 'Don't you worry. It'll keep to the morning, sure. Just go on up. Big Liam and me won't be far behind you. You can tell me all about it tomorrow.'

Liam gave his mum a brief outline before he followed his granda. He didn't mention the twitch & his granda going on about it but. More ammunition that would only be. For his da.

The big light was on & his granda was putting his pyjama top on when Liam stepped into the room. He paused, wondering should he go back out. 'Come on ahead, youngfella,' his granda said but. 'Don't mind me. Just get on wi whatever you have to do.'

He got on with it. His granda even saw him in his undies.

This time, the light stayed on till the old boy had finished his prayers. Liam didn't mind but. He just lay there just, thinking about

Carfin & feeling pleased about it. He'd got his granda back, it felt lik. All they'd seen, heard, & done together was amazing.

'Night-night, son,' his granda said.

'Night, Granda,' he answered.

When the light clicked off, he said some prayers of his own, Liam. He prayed for peace in Derry. Peace in Northern Ireland. Peace among the McCluskeys. Then John came back to mind & he made him his special intention.

Father, Son, Holy Ghost. Amen.

He shuffled till he got himself comfortable.

As he lay listening to the silence—his granda wasn't snoring yet—his thoughts drifted back to the Robertson youngfella. Beginning to wonder what three mentions & above all a girlfriend would be lik, Liam was, when his eyes closed & he drifted over.

the secret of how to love

What chance had—or *have*—I?

My da—in front of my mum once—told me he didn't love her. 'Your mum knows and understands this, don't you?' Mum's eyes agreed. Were too worn out to dissent.

The one woman he loved was his mother.

'Your uncle Kevin's the same. He *decided* to love your aunt Maureen. Ask him, if you don't believe me. He told me so himself sure. Is a liar if he tells you different.'

My da was 'the only brother never to lift his hand.' Prided himself on it. 'The rest of them *did*. Paddy—even—did. I'm the only one didn't. Whatever else I may've done, I never touched your mother. Isn't that right, love?'

Today, a year, a good year, after the funeral, I find a file.

Useful Quotes.

And between

There is only one thing impossible to God—
He cannot refuse His Mother anything
(St Anselm)

and

Without Mary it is difficult to succeed;
with Mary it is impossible to fail
(Maximilian Kolbe)

this:

Love is not a feeling.
It is an act of will.

Anonymous, I take it.

kenny ryan
1976

Word got round that someone'd been appointed & that the man who got the job was from Derry. It was nothing that would've affected Kenny Ryan. You wouldn't have expected him to hear even. Lo 'n' behold he did but & one Sunday, after ten Mass, didn't he pounce on our Liam.

'Are you Mr. O'Donnell?'

Liam said he was.

'And are you a Derry man, as people are saying?'

Liam said he was.

Satisfied, Kenny said he was too. Was from Derry originally 'n' all.

'You're kidding?! What's your name? I'd be lying if I said I recognised ye.'

Even when Kenny told him, our Liam couldn't place him. The only Ryans he knew were from Cable Street & he couldn't see this boy being anything to themmins.

He said to Kenny to come up for his dinner anyhow. The boy, after all, was on his own.

'What now?'

'Of course, now! Just come. There's more than enough to go round!'

Kenny relented & they turned to go. Had hardly reached the brow of the hill but before Liam'd to stop to clarify something.

'On one condition: it's Liam, Kenny. Forget the Mr. O'Donnell.'

The dog growled, baring his teeth, when Kenny first walked in.

'That's enough of that, you!' Liam hit him a slap.

Bridget, hearing a stranger, took a quick look in from the kitchen. 'This is my wife, Bridget. Kenny's from Derry originally 'n' all,' Liam told her. 'He's a Ryan. Nothing to the ones on Cable Street but! I said we'd give him his dinner!'

Bridget said, 'Aye—no bother!' and shook Kenny's hand. 'Nice to meet you, Kenny!'

Next job to do was introduce the weans: from Liam down to wee Orla.

'Seven, you have?'

Kenny made some comment their da shrugged off: 'It's right enough what they say, sure—it's cheaper by the dozen!'

Annette was clinging to the dog still. There was still the odd angry growl.

'Cut that out, you!' Big Liam warned. 'Or it's another slap you'll be gettin!'

How long are you over in Scotland? wasn't straightforward in Kenny's case. He'd been back in Scotland for the last ten years. Was out of Derry over thirty.

All over, the boy had been: Pakistan, India—you name it. Walking everywhere, too! First few times he visited, he was always on about Turkey. Seems there was nowhere in Turkey Kennyboy didn't know, not that the same one was for letting on how come. He took great delight in describing the massages: how you lay face down & a boy walked up you, footing it up your spine. Seeing our Liam looking sceptical, Kenny got up to demonstrate. 'You'd be surprised,' he insisted, 'what good it does!' Taking dainty wee footsteps towards the fire.

He could've been Turkish himself, nearly, Kenny. Had a face that was made for a skull cap, that wouldn't've stood out in a bazaar. There was something about his colouring 'n' all, that dated back to his travels maybe. The main thing about him but was: how incredibly neat the boy was. He maybe wasn't the tallest of men, was a great one but for a suit. His shoes ye could see yer face in. His hair, never long, he always brylcreemed back. He was wild well-spoken for a factory worker. In fact: ye'd never've known he was Derry born 'n' bred, if he hadn't told ye himself.

The boy was thon way, it was hard to say what age he was. He must've been fifty at least but, when he first turned up in the house. Not that the same one looked it. No, Kenny Ryan looked after himself. Or *looked* lik he did. Which is why the O'Donnells were all so shocked when he said where he bought all his clothes. Every bloody stitch was from the Barras.

'You're not telling me you buy your shoes there 'n' all?'

For once, our Liam was speechless.

'I do,' Kenny confirmed. 'Why wouldn't I?'

He took one off and handed it over.

Big Liam was giving it: 'Clothes, I can imagine. Clothes, you can wash or dry-clean. I couldn't see myself wearing secondhand shoes but—' when Kenny interrupted him.

'Inspect them then!' he demanded—ye could tell but his feelings were hurt but.

'The best of leather!' he insisted as Liam read the writing. 'Leather soles *and* uppers. An old shilling, they cost me!'

'Can't argue wi that!' Liam conceded.

Sunday dinner became a regular occurrence. Before too long, it was weekly.

The weans would look forward to him coming. To begin wi, sure, they were curious & he did, after all, bring them sweets. Saying that: it was well seen he'd no weans of his own. Week after week, his *varieties* started a riot, nearly. Would've done, probably, if it hadn't've been for Liam. Big Liam, I mean. 'Yous know what'll happen, if I catch yous fighting!' he'd warn. 'The whole buckin lot'll go in the bin!'

'Say thank you to Mr. Ryan!' he'd then insist as the Flake, Aztec, Mars bar, etc. went off in separate directions.

It must've been after the clothes conversation Kenny first turned up on a Saturday. On his way *back* from the Barras.

He plonked a strange purchase down in the middle of the floor.

'Does anyone know what that is?' he asked the assembled O'Donnells.

'Haven't the foggiest!' our Liam admitted. The weans all shook their heads just.

The one thing they did know was: that this was bloomin boring.

'Is it from the inside of a machine?' Sean asked.

'Could it be part of a broken lawnmower?' Ciara sounded confident.

Kenny said no to both, cut poor wee Cahal short.

'You're approaching it all wrong!' he insisted. 'No more guesses! Ask me questions to try and narrow it down. Do you know *Twenty Questions* on the wireless? The first question's always: is it animal, vegetable or mineral? That's how to start. Animal, vegetable or mineral—and take it from there . . .'

The weans were out of their depth, weren't in the least bit interested. Kennyboy was lucky if he got to question three.

'Just tell us, Kenny!' the wee ones pleaded.

He wasn't for giving in but, insisted they'd to guess. Yet more proof it was: he was a dead loss wi weans. One by one they wandered off just—leaving Kenny alone wi the dog. An' his unidentified mysterious bloody object abandoned just on the floor.

It was every Saturday evening after that. Every Saturday night & Sunday lunchtime. Bridget, fed up managing, started to count him in.

He appreciated her, Kenny, at least. Week after week, he brought her a Fry's Cream—handing it over lik he was giving the woman gold. A running joke, it became: that Kenny Ryan idolised her. To be fair: there was nothing the same boy wouldn't have done for our Liam's Bridget. Anything that broke, Kenny fixed. Cassette recorders, hair driers, you name it. The weans' trannies. The record player. He saved them a fortune in repairs!

Be that as it may: Bridget was still at her wit's end when Kenny started coming a third night. Wednesday was his half day, he revealed. An' always he would go to Paddy's Market.

Saturdays & Sundays—the Barras.

Wednesdays—Paddy's Market.

The smell, the *dirt,* off the stuff was unreal & Bridget would be cooking the tea too! An' it wasn't as if Liam was home to entertain him.

Bridget, as ye might imagine, was completely browned off.

The weans, God love them, had their homeworks to do.

One time Bridget looked in, Kenny was playing wi the dog.

Even the buckin dog showed no reaction.

It was Young Liam who started to ask questions.

Annette & Ciara were in on it 'n' all.

'K.R.' they'd started calling him. Not to his face but.

At fifteen, fourteen, thirteen, they were starting to have minds of their own, & Kenny'd made the mistake of totally offending them. It was one night the news was on & somewhere in America, a boy was due to be executed. Was the first our Liam's weans had heard of death row & the girls & young Liam were appalled. Kenny, needless to say but, was all for it. For Kenny, the electric chair was *too good for the boy*. Kenny'd've cut his hands off—lik they done in countries lik Turkey. Thrown him into a cell & left him to rot.

'I take it you're in favour of bringing back the birch?'

Young Liam was fizzing. Ye could hear it.

'I am!' Kenny insisted. Bugger wasn't for budging.

Listening to the guy was bad enough. The day the boy was executed but, the lousy shite "dropped by."

Dropped by, their arse! There was no way, that night, the weans could be polite.

It was Annette who gave the signal & off they headed.

'That boy's pure sick!' she hissed. 'That's what he is: sick!'

'He's a slimey oul so-and-so!'—Ciara. 'Don't be upsettin yourself, Annette—he's not worth it.'

'Who's he, like, to judge?' Liam suddenly gave it.

Whatever way Ciara reacted, a penny'd just dropped. This was what Miss Rafferty was always stressing: you had to think critically, had to be willing to challenge.

Something in Annette's face was urging Liam on.

'What I want to know is *why*?' he said. 'Why's he not married? Why's he no family?'

'Why's nobody heard of him?'—Annette.

'Why'd he leave Ireland?'—Liam again. 'Why India 'n' Turkey? Why bloomin *walking*?'

'What age d'ye think he is?' Ciara interrupted.

'Don't know. Fifty-something? Dad's in his forties, sure!'

Ciara'd got Liam thinking: 'Born in nineteen-twentysomething, that would make him. So: nineteen or twenty when the war ended . . .'

'D'ye think he was a soldier?'—Annette.

'Can't see it.'—Liam. 'The navy, if anything.'

'So he went to all them countries after the war?'

'Reckon so. I can see him walkin 'n' walkin—I can't see him fightin but. Can *you*?'

The girls shook their heads.

'So that was the 1950s 'n' then he came to Scotland?'—Ciara.

'Would add up, aye.'

'I wonder what the reason was? How he didn't go back to Ireland?'

They were onto something, it felt lik. An' getting a bit of revenge for the guy on death row.

Their da, it turned out, had been asking questions 'n' all. Had been *putting out feelers* whenever he phoned Derry.

None of their aunts 'n' uncles had ever heard tell of Kenny.

Their gran 'n' all her pals had never heard tell of him either.

Christy, an uncle by marriage, it was, who finally came up wi the goods. Karate & amateur boxing were the crucial connection.

Karate, you could see. He'd that kind of frame, Kenny. Boxing was harder to imagine.

It was the training that appealed, he told our Liam. It kept you off the street & out of trouble. 'And there was no shortage of trouble back in those days!'

Running up Rosemount *backwards* was what Kenny minded most. Murder, he said it was.

'But a heck of a lot better than getting *involved*.'

('He means the IRA,' Liam'd to explain to his sisters.)

It wasn't long after that conversation Christy was back on the blower. He'd more information. This time, even better.

On three different occasions, he told them, Kenny'd been due to get married.

An' on three different occasions, he'd jilted the girl at the altar.

Three bloody times, the so-and-so failed to show. That was why he scampered, Christy had discovered: the "boys" were after him.

('No, not his fiancée's brothers,' Liam explained this time. 'The *Provos*!')

There was more! Two of Kenny's cousins lived in Derry still. An aunt did 'n' all. All three were women, ages wi Kenny maybe. *Delighted* they were, to have found him. *Keen as anything* to meet him.

'They're after his buckin dough,' said Uncle Christy—who knew about the money down the cushions.

Our Liam, being our Liam, invited the three of them over.

'Tell them they're very welcome,' he told Christy to tell them. 'Any time they lik! They're more than welcome in our house!'

There wasn't a hope in hell of Kenny issuing invites. That, our Liam didn't have to be told.

The boy had a room 'n' kitchen, it seems. Single-storey, mid-terrace, bit of a garden to the front. His own front door, at least, as the two Liams told us. What the problem was was: it was crammed full wi junk. A mini Barras, lik. Four bloody motorbikes, seemingly, were parked round the room. His bed folded down from the wall. Stuff was piled high everywhere, the shelves chock-a-block round the walls. You'd to jump over a hole to get into the kitchen. The toilet was off that again. Big Liam even turned a cuppa down even—after seeing the state of the dishcloths.

The other thing to come out that day was: Kenny Ryan had *rats*. He'd hear them—imagine!—at night & fling a buckin hammer at them.

On one famous occasion, he split one's head open.

Back to the big reunion but: Kenny, when he got wind of it, was raging. So buckin raging, he couldn't begin to disguise it.

Liam's three oldest were rubbing their hands in glee.

'NO WAY, Liam!' Kenny roared. 'I don't want to see them.'

'It's too late, Kenny!' their da informed him. 'The ladies are already on their way. I don't know what you're worrying about. You can meet them here, if you lik.'

The fact it wasn't at his place seemed to help.

The evening, in the end-up, passed without incident.

Not wanting to miss nothing, the weans ensured they were in.

Lik *This Is Your Life*, it was! 'All the way from Londonderry, it's your cousins, Annie & Rosie—and your aunt, Deirdre!'

There was a strained politeness. The ladies—middle-aged, overweight, all done up in their corsets—were given the settee. Kenny, the closest armchair. The O'Donnells watched lik hawks until finally, eventually, Kenny thawed. The ladies, all smiles, suggested a photo.

Our Liam took some that Kenny even smiled for—squeezing in between his cousins even.

The strain there was before had gone. The strange politeness stayed but.

Christy 'n' our Liam had never had so much to talk about.

There was one last thing Liam was desperate to know.

'Would you say it was okay, Christy, to leave him in charge of your house?'

'What were you thinkin lik, Liam?'

'Well, we're due to be over home for three weeks—an' the last couple of times, I put the dog in the kennels. I could save a tiny fortune if Kenny house-sat. Wha' d'ye think? Should I ask him?'

'Well, he wouldn't run off wi yir daughters, that's for sure!'

'They're coming with me 'n' Bridget. So too are the boys.'

'No, seriously, Liam: I think you're okay. I'd say he's straight 'n' honest. No one I've spoken to has suggested any different.'

'Aye, you're probably right, Christy. Speakin of which: did I tell ye the story from his work?'

'Don't think so. Though ye said he was working, aye—'

'I'll have to tell you this one before I hang up! Seems he went in to work one Monday there an' the foreman was calling him for everything. They'd overpaid him on the Friday an' he'd not had the decency to say. Kenny took so much of it, it seems, before—finally—he erupted. "The reason I haven't said anything is I've yet to open the envelope," he told them. "Expect me to believe that?" the foreman sneered. "You will," Kenny told him 'n' stormed out. First thing next morning, he's up at the office, handing back their pay packet. "YOU open it," says Kenny. "YOU check it." An' here—before the boy can do anything, he takes out a second envelope. An' a third 'n' a fourth 'n' a fifth—every single one of them unopened. Nine there were on the table, apparently, before Kennyboy was finished.'

'Take it he got an apology?' Christy pretended to ask. 'Give him the keys of your house, Liam!'

Soon after that, the O'Donnells were over in Derry. The story of Kenny's pay packets had beaten them to it. Was just as buckin well the guy had fled to Scotland. The whole o bloody Derry wanted to burgle him.

The call came on the Monday—before the weans had settled even. Kenny phoned their Gran's, to speak to their da.

'It's the dog,' Liam announced, coming back in from the hall. 'Wrecked the buckin house, he has.'

Annette's face dropped. There was nothing the wean could do but.

'When Kenny got back last night, the place looked lik a bomb had hit it. The two curtains were down an' so was the pelmet. The very bit of wood the curtain rail was nailed to was snapped in two.'

'That wasn't a bomb, Liam! Sounds more lik an army job to me, hi! Ye sure ye weren't raided?'

Liam glared at the jokester. 'I can do wi'out the wise cracks, nephew!'

He turned to Bridget.

'The settee's ripped to shreds, love. We'll need a whole new suite—"

Bridget didn't speak.

'Labradors!' Liam cursed. 'Don't any of yis ever get one! That's the third buckin settee I'm having to buy!'

'An' what about Shamrock, Dad?' Was Annette dared to ask.

'It's into the kennels wi him. I told Kenny to take him. What else was I supposed to say?' he protested, spotting Bridget's reaction.

'Do you want the *good* news?' he went on.

Bridget nodded.

'He's caught the mouse—'

'Have yis a mouse?' someone asked.

'Not any more!'

'How'd he catch it, Dad?'—Sean.

'He used chocolate biscuits!'

'Thought so!'—Sean again.

'He crushed up a digestive, seemingly, an' mixed it wi Polyfilla—'

'Jesus, Liam! Where'd he get that recipe?'

'It's what he gives his rats!' the weans chorused.

Was either that or the flying hammer, it seems.

'The Polyfilla sets in their stomachs,' Sean explained. 'The weight of it slows them down an' they can't get back out through the holes.'

'Someone's been paying attention!' Christy laughed. 'D'ye pay attention lik that at school?'

The three weeks flew past just. Suddenly it was time to go back.

Bridget's heart sank when she saw the state of her kitchen. He hadn't lifted a finger, Kenny hadn't. Hadn't bothered his arse to clean at all. The same plate & cup had been used for three weeks. Same bits of cutlery 'n' all. The *Fairy* buckin *Liquid* had taken root.

The room he'd slept in was even worse even. Bridget had cleared the older girls' bedroom out specially, seemingly. Fixed it up nice. It was the smell that hit her first, she said, when she went to change it back. The window'd not been opened in all them weeks. Nor had the dirty bugger changed the bed. The pillowcase was clatty wi Brylcreem. St. Veronica's veil or the Turin shroud wouldn't've had a bloody look in, apparently. She'd ended up burning the pillowcase, Bridget. Two of her best sheets 'n' buckin all.

Her one consolation was: there was no more bloody mouse.

***

Fast-forward thirty-odd years. Liam, God rest him, is four years dead now.

Kenny's been gone twenty—at buckin least.

His house—would ye credit it?—is still lying empty.

Ye'd think someone would do something. That someone would be responsible. But *no* but.

Rottin away it is. You wouldn't buy in the street even.

All thon stuff from the Barras is probably in there 'n' all still. Stuff he always insisted he'd re-sell.

Most of the bloody stuff he never fixed.

At some point—in the eighties maybe—Kenny's visits stopped.

By that stage, boyfriends 'n' girlfriends were in 'n' out of the house, sure.

Maybe it felt too crowded. Maybe he felt neglected.

However thick-skinned, he maybe picked up vibes maybe.

His visits dried up anyway—whatever the reason.

The last years of his life he spent caretaking.

A caravan site it was & he'd no sooner started work there than he started to sleep in his office.

To cut down on the travel, he said.

'To save the flippin bus fares!' the O'Donnells chorused.

A good ten years maybe, he lived lik that.

There were nights wi winds & rains when ye couldn't help thinking of him.

There was no call for it either: the whole buckin time, he'd thon wee house still.

Not long after his da died, young Liam fancied a walk one day—round the dam and up the Braes, lik he'd liked to walk in his teens.

Bridget, to his delight, said she'd join him.

On their way back, they were, when they passed Kenny's street.

'Do you mind, Mum, what number he was?'

Bridget didn't. Not that it took them long to find it.

Neither Liam or Bridget said anything, it seems. They both just stopped & stood there just. The garden *screamed* neglect. Animal, vegetable, mineral—it was all there. Pigeons & seagulls were picking at somebody's vomit. The carcass of a bird lay at the door. What looked lik a rag-tree was taller than the house, got. The weeds & nettles had completely taken over. The guy's powerbox, even, had slowly rusted away. Its front prised open, the wiring now in shreds. The house itself had slumped, apparently—the FOR SALE sign barely upright behind a broken pane.

Liam, seeing this, could imagine the rats now just.

He turned to Bridget to say so. Her head but was lowered. Her hands, joined in prayer.

'You alright, Mum?' he asked once she finished.

She nodded.

'May God rest his soul,' she said. Then turned to head home.

we now know

It's hard to know where to start. To say where it all started.

What I know now, I only suspected back then:

—that it went on before me

—that I wasn't the first

—that he worked his way down the rest before—finally—reaching me.

Whether or not me brother knew, I don't know. Kevin wasted no time in getting out of the house but, that's for sure. First, the junior seminary. Later, the Forces. Before the Troubles, it was.

Whether or not he knew's a different matter.

Maybe he scarpered cos he did.

Or maybe me da done something to him 'n' all.

Me sisters, it turns out, *did* talk about it.

Me mother, of course, was in Granshaw.

His classic was to ask you to scrub his back. To wash his back in the bath. When he asked you to do that, your time was coming. Josephine will tell you that. Patricia will tell you that 'n' all. Margaret could too, no doubt. I know for a fact Bernadette could.

'It's okay: I'll wear me trunks!' he'd assure you. Obvious *now*, it is. Without anyone opening their mouths, he was on the defensive.

Credit where credit's due: he put trunks on. They stayed on 'n' all. Wasn't as if he was up to something. Not initially anyway. He'd lean forward just & let Josephine, or Patricia, or whichever girl it was, get on with it.

Don't ask me why me mother didn't do it. Maybe at one point she did. She'll have had her reasons.

She's not in Granshaw without reason, of course.

It was me father, whoever saw him, put her there.

It seems he'd always his trunks still on when he got out. Was lik people do at the beach: he wrapped a towel round. And if Josephine, say, was still there, he done what he'd do at the beach: worked the trunks down under the towel, then let them fall to the floor.

Nothing wrong with that, you might say—till the first time the towel fell. The day it accidentally (supposedly) slipped. Josephine, Patricia, Margaret, Bernadette—all four of them over in Scotland now—can tell you that.

Ye can imagine what came next.

It was probably deliberate on his part—*grooming*'s the word for it these days. All them times it was just about scrubbing his back! Nothing else. Nothing to raise an eyebrow. So each of them, in turn, drops her guard—if she had one. An' that's the moment he pounces.

'O Jesus!' he'd stammer, pretending to be flustered, snatching the towel from the floor. 'Sorry, love!'

Next thing you knew, he was justifying it.

This way, when you got married, you'd know what your husband looked lik. Ye were better knowing than not. Sparing you a fright on your wedding night, he was. Your mother, God love her, hadn't. Known.

Me ma knew what he was up to. Why else did she end up in Granshaw?

She screamed out of her, it seems, when Josephine, the eldest, said to her.

You can imagine what it felt lik for Josephine when he turned his attentions to Patricia. An' for Josephine & Patricia, both, when he turned his attentions to Margaret.

It's far worse, sometimes, when it's someone else it's happening to.

Seems he was faithful—if that's the word—to whichever girl he was onto. Once he dropped to the next one, that was you.

Bernadette was the final straw. Her being that bit younger.

The age gap, it seems, done the older ones' heads in—so Josephine said to my mother.

Kevin was well gone by that stage. Still got the postcards, we have, from the different places he was stationed in.

Bernadette was the only one to scream, they say, first time he done what he done to her.

I mind the night fine. *Top of the Pops* was on. Mungo Jerry were No. 1. Not that I knew what he was up to.

He told me she'd seen a mouse when, eventually, he came back down.

'Did ye catch it?'

'That's what kept me!'

They hadn't reckoned on him turning to me, it seems.

The youngest.

The only other boy.

I'll hold me hand up & admit it: even before he started, I'd lost the plot. He warned me often enough. The odd clip round the ear but, or slap wherever he caught me, was water off a duck's back just.

It wasn't even defiance.

I wasn't always a rogue. Maybe it was me ma being in Granshaw. Maybe I was missing her maybe—not that I ever admitted it.

Or maybe I was responding to vibes.

Ye got explanations for nothing. 'Gi'e ma head peace, would ye!'—as much of an answer as ye got.

The night the pigs brought me home—accompanied by the Brits, to protect them—was the night me da lost it.

'*I'll* deal with this!' he assured the pig who spoke.

'He'll be sorry alright when I'm done wi him!'

'He'll not sit down for a week!'

The pig seemed satisfied & left. The boy wi the rifle nodded too.

The door was hardly closed when he went beserk. 'Bed!' he roared. 'An' do you see this here?' he said, unbuckling the wee narrow belt he wore. 'I'm comin up in a minute 'n' I'm going tay bait the livin daylights out o ye!'

'Trousers off!' he roared after me. 'Ye'll feel it this time okay! Police 'n' buckin army at me door! I'm warnin ye now: the trousers had better be off!'

It was more than a minute. Ten, more lik.

What he wasn't to know—or maybe he did—was: I'd no underpants. The arse was out of the only pair I had. An' wi me ma in Granshaw, there was no one to buy new ones. No trousers meant no nothing.

I was crying, waiting even. Down below was swollen, not that I knew the reason. The one thing I did know was: he wasn't to see it. I tried putting a pyjama top on—Kevin's before he left. It was soaked wi snot and tears in no time.

Me mickey was going back to normal, nearly, when the stairs started to creak.

I headed for the fireplace, to hide it.

He came in, saw me, snorted. There I was, sure: arms along the mantelpiece; me behind pointing out, waiting for it.

'Wha' d'ye think it is—*Tom Brown's Schooldays*?' he sneered.

There was a strong smell of drink off him there hadn't been before.

He came up behind me & snapped the belt. I knew without looking it was folded in two. He'd the buckle & the holes end in one fist, the middle of the leather in the other.

I was praying he wouldn't use the buckle when he spotted the way me mickey was.

'Ya dirty wee bugger!' he said, reaching for me. He turned me round by the ear. 'Wha' d'ye call that?'

'I'm bustin for the toilet!' I tried to claim.

He threw me into the grate just about, he was so disgusted.

'Well you're naw going nowhere till I've finished wi ye—'

I don't know whether I heard or felt it first. It was agony, anyway, that's for sure, the way the belt caught me.

'That's me warming up just,' he announced. 'That one doesn't count.'

After a few lik thon—was lik he let the pain fade before delivering the next—he started counting aloud.

I danced a jig as each one connected.

Screaming & pleading didn't help. He just kept going just.

When he got to *thir*-teen, *four*-teen, I thought he'd never stop.

I dropped to the floor when he did.

'Well?' he demanded.

'I'm sorry, Da!' I sobbed.

'I should think so too!' he said. 'Bringing them buckin sods to my door!'

'Wha' else d'ye say?' he suddenly insisted.

I looked at him, lost.

'Thank you, Da!' he said.

I twigged immediately. Was lik on TV.

'Thank you, Da!' I dutifully repeated.

Big buckin shite wasn't for leaving. Not wanting to anger him, I decided to stay where I was. He watched me nursing the marks—the ones I could reach.

When he did finally go, he was no time away before he was back. Stinking of whisky, this time.

He sat himself down on Kevin's bed.

Still watching me, he was. Lik a hawk.

'Have ye learned your lesson?' he asked eventually.

I nodded.

'I don't hear you—'

'I have, Da, aye—'

'Come over 'n' give me a hug then.'

I hugged him. He let me.

'That hurt me more than it hurt you,' he said.

It went from that to him kissing it better. The weight of him pinning me down as he tended the welts.

It went from that to me seeing a grown man's mickey & what it can do, all.

There was nothing to be ashamed of, he assured me. I'd be a grown man too one day.

That was only the first time. It certainly wasn't the last.

I gave him no more reason to beat me. The rest of that night, but, got repeated & repeated & repeated. For a while, I thought nothing of it. The fear somehow went. Weirdly, I started to lik it.

It wasn't ideal. Definitely wasn't right. It was affection but. For once, he was showing me affection.

Some time later, something changed.

It was in me head it happened.

I wanted to kiss a girl & it was as if I couldn't do it wi this going on.

For the first time ever, I understood our Kevin.

Part of me wanted to kick hell out of him—me da, that is.

Too much of a lightweight I was but.

When I did do something, it was something else I done.

I felt lik a traitor even considering it. Even more of a traitor actually doing it.

It got to the point but where I approached a priest but.

***

'Aw, Jesus, Mary & St Joseph!' Father said in his southern accent, when I told him what was happening.

Was lik I'd stabbed him with a knife, the way his voice went.

Was lik: he'd heard this kind of story before.

Was lik: this wasn't the first time he'd saved someone.

'Come here over, youngfella!' he said.

He put his arm round me. Only let go of me to pray.

It was all in Latin. I only knew he'd finished cos he blissed himself.

'Tell me every ting you need to,' he urged.

There was kindness in his voice. Not lik from the pulpit on Sundays.

'No holding back now, Lawrence. Don't be being embarrassed. God, in His infinite wisdom, will understand.'

I poured my heart out.

There was something about his eyes, close up. The teetotal smell of his breath.

I confessed to the moments of enjoyment even.

That—likewise—went through him.

He'd have to purify me, he announced, lifting down a folder.

He'd get the Holy Water.

I thought nothing of it. Me mother, I knew, was *churched*. After each & every birth, the priest had churched her.

It meant she could go to Communion again. Could go in the front door.

Father returned with Lourdes Water; opened the leather folder; found the section he needed.

'Drop your trousers, child,' he said.

I hesitated, naturally. Me mother would be black affronted: the priest seeing we couldn't afford underclothing.

'It's important to apply it directly,' he explained.

He showed me where it said it, in Latin.

There was no reason for alarm. It wasn't as if he touched me. Naw, he sprinkled it from where he was standing just, his eyes closed as he prayed. I closed mine too. The Latin instantly cleansed me.

When he was done, he seemed to hesitate. Then, consulting the big folder, he spun me round.

'Your back passage too, son!' he insisted.

He made it sound necessary. Your body as God's Temple.

I bent to let him. I had to. You didn't say boo in them days.

When I tried to straighten up, he put his hand on my back.

Still praying, he was, I took it.

Then I heard his zip. Him fumbling.

His up was the size of me da's down. Done all the same things but.

Priest or no priest, it was the same buckin story.

For a long time, he had me in his grip. I'd to keep my mouth shut, to do what he said, he said. He threatened to tell me da all I told him. The day would come, he warned, when I'd need a reference. Me passport photo signed.

I tried to steer clear of him.

Course, he accused me of avoiding him, first time he caught me on the street.

I followed him back to the Chapel House, afraid of any fuss.

He done what he done every other time. Only harder.

His other trick was to visit the house. He was looking for a volunteer, he'd say. A *good strong youngfella.*

Me da would call me down.

'Not at all, Father!' I'd hear him say. 'Don't be paying out money. Our Lawrence will help ye!'

'Keeps them off the streets, eh?' he'd say, winking, as the priest led me out.

We'd hardly be in the door before he'd the trousers off me.

The housekeeper was never to be seen.

With him, I never enjoyed it. I didn't want to be close.

Didn't stop him but. 'There's noan like ye!' he'd say.

After all that practice wi me da, it was no wonder.

They taught us at school once that priests also confess.

They also sin. Are also human.

Each has his own confessor. The bishop maybe.

It went on long enough. One way or another, he'd seek me out.

There were other youngfellas too, we now know. The occasional weegirl also.

Sixty-five percent male, thirty-five female, are the figures in his statement.

He only gave me peace after he seen me wi Rosemary Hanlon.

Must've thought we were sweethearts.

I'd yet to even kiss her. He must've been afraid I'd tell her everything but.

Was me got the Law onto him. Not then but. Now. Just recently there. All these years later.

This time, I told a social worker & chose the fella carefully.

Me luck was in. Ciaran, thank God, can keep his trousers up.

He's been spot-on, Ciaran. Went straight to the top. And when the bishop failed to act, he wasn't slow in returning. Threatened to involve the press, he did.

That's what he done 'n' all! When all the bishop done was transfer the canon, Ciaran went straight to the papers.

He found some journalist who lives, breathes, and sleeps Jesus.

That's their motivation. It's not against the Church. It's *for* Jesus. *For* the church they love—

Whatever! Long as no one else suffers what I done.

There was one other victim in all of this. Kevin.

IRA got him.

Coming back home was the mistake he made.

Years ago now. Troubles were at their peak.

Made an example of him, they did.
This was what would happen to anyone joining the army.
If only he'd stayed in the seminary.
Troubles had yet to start, of course, when he left.

Father Bradley. Father Kevin. Sometimes I try to imagine it.

As for me da: he's shitting himself. Is feart we could still report him.
He gets nowhere near his grandweans. Course not.
He tried to cast up my shenanigans wi the priest once.
'Zip it, Da!' I told him. 'If ye know what's good for you, zip it!'
He has to have a drink in him to open his mouth now.

Me mother, God love her, is still in Granshaw.

The girls have got their own lives. Me ma misses them, I just hope
they're happy but.
That what went on in the house is in the past now.

As for me: people are doing their best.
Ciaran says: wi God's Holy help, I'll make it. He's got prayer
groups—all over—praying for me.
It'll take time, he says. A lot of prayer.
Aye, I have to be patient just, different ones tell me.
Putting pen to paper is maybe a start.

There's no denying it, right enough: people are trying to help me.
I'm no further forward but, if ye ask me.
If ye ask me, I'm no further forward.

a limit

In the last year of the last Labour Government—*Old* Labour, that is, Labour-Labour—Liam, the first in the family to do so, went to university to be taught—by a Derryman, as it happens—that the most important question is *Why?* That's what ye should ask yourself every time, the guy insisted: *Why?* Why did the author do this, include this? *For they had their reasons, you know. They weren't stupid. These things didn't just happen by chance.*

The Derryman—who minded Liam of his uncle Eugene, minded him but at the same time didn't but—repeated that question throughout the year & each time looked at the class & laughed: a laugh that broke out from behind his glasses & over his moustache, a laugh that was maybe nervous, maybe embarrassed, maybe a mixture. Or maybe the boy was genuinely amused maybe. Found it genuinely funny that this was the question ye always had to ask. That there was no escaping it. That ye couldn't always answer it. That *he* got to introduce it to one year-group after another. Whatever. It was only when his off-centre laugh faded, anyhow, that ye might've focused on what he was wearing again. His checked shirt. And brown cords.

Why? was the first question to ask yourself every morning, according to one of his colleagues 'n' all. The one who identified a *Bounty advert scenario* in many a poem. If ye could answer that question positively, this lecturer said, ye wouldn't top yourself.

When Liam started going abroad, the question folk seemed to ask themselves there was *Why should I?* It wasn't that they were upstarts, cranks, or arrogant even. That they were selfish gits or shites. Naw: they just had to be *persuaded* that whatever-it-was made sense. Was worthy of their time & effort. Fitted in wi what they were about. That whoever-it-was who was wanting whatever didn't have a bloody cheek, wasn't pulling a fast one, was prepared to show them respect, to allow them a say in the matter—a real say.

Sometimes, even then, Liam would step onto an escalator in Munich, say & there'd be a German guy & his girlfriend ahead of him or even just people going to their work & Liam would envy them their way of doing things, the way they'd grown up, the non-existence of certain issues, of things that got in the way. The *space* these people had been allowed. Were allowed. The space they *ex-pected*.

The French, one French pal told him, would just say 'Stuff this for a lark!' Were great ones for *Je m'en fous*, and fuck the consequences. Their government knew it 'n' all. Knew there was always the chance whole sections of the population could stop, down tools, & tell them where to go. They wouldn't worry about what could follow either. Wouldn't give a toss. Naw—the French, François said, had their government trained. It knew there was a limit.

mrs. goodman
Sheffield, England

She's whatever age she is, Mrs. Goodman, and keeps herself to herself. All them years she lived opposite me, sure, it was like: blink and ye'd miss her. Well over ten years we must've been neighbours and I swear to God: ye wouldn't need both hands to count how often we spoke. Her front porch was about your only chance—if she struggled with the lock. Either that or ye'd run into her on the lane, maybe, and say hello and offer to carry her bag. Saying that, it was a case of: speak and she'd answer ye. A polite wee woman, she is. Very civil. *Proper*, even.

What we knew about her till recently there wasn't much at all. Her husband was the local dentist, and a kinder man ye couldn't've wished for, but he's dead a good fifteen years now, Dr. Goodman. Their twins—identical, boys—were in the same form at school as Mrs. Cline's eldest. The fifties, it would've been. Early sixties at the latest. Mrs. Cline still goes on, to this day, about the time her youngfella was asked round. For afternoon tea, it was, and only children learning German could go. The Goodman boys themselves weren't doing German but their mother asked them to invite the ones who were. Wasn't that strange, I suppose. She wanted to encourage the German scholars just, with her being from Klagenfurt—ye call the place—originally. Mrs. Cline's boy still minds the books she showed them. The funny script. Ye wouldn't've got books lik thon here then, sure. Not in them days. All the biggest names, it was too! The German Shakespeares. Not that the boys would've understood a word of it at that point. One, right enough, went on to teach. And who knows, maybe that cup of tea, that invitation that day, had a hand in it.

There's no denying: we knew next to nothing, right enough. And wouldn't have begun to suspect the stuff that's coming out now. Charlotte Soyfer, it was, who googled her. Run into Mrs. Goodman on the bus, she had—late June or early July, it would've been—and her bags gave away where she'd been. Shopping! Best of shops too! Boutiques, if you don't mind!

'Been treating yourself, dear?' Mrs. Soyfer asked.

'Yes,' says Mrs. Goodman, with the warmest of smiles. (It's a really sweet smile the woman has. Despite all that happened to her.)

'You do right to!' Mrs. Soyfer said.

'Who else will, if you don't?' she nearly added, she told me. She remembered just in time, though: the woman's a widow.

'Have you something special coming up then?' she asked instead.

A graduation, if you don't mind, the "something" was.

'Don't tell me your grandson's graduating already?' Mrs. Soyfer replied.

She knew about the eldest twin's Edward from a previous conversation.

'No, it's not Edward, it's me!' was the answer she got.

Imagine!

'I didn't know you were studying, dear,' was all Mrs. Soyfer could say, she was so flabbergasted.

'You're right—I haven't been,' Mrs. Goodman admitted. 'It's an honorary degree.'

Mrs. Soyfer, by this stage, of course, was desperate to hear more. Sod's law though: next stop was Mrs. Goodman's.

'You'll have to excuse me,' she said, preparing to go. 'I'll tell you all about it another time.'

'See and enjoy it, dear, if I don't see you before!' Mrs. Soyfer said. 'Oh—and congratulations!' she called after her, realising she hadn't congratulated the woman.

Was only as she settled back in her seat, she realised too, she hadn't been offered the slightest peek at what the woman had bought. A very private wee woman, as I say.

Needless to say: Charlotte Soyfer was no time in the door that night than she'd her husband's computer on. Ye want to see the number of pages there is with Mrs. Goodman's name! Hits, Mrs. Soyfer called them—like she was some kind of pop star. I know buck all about computers, me. Won't go near them—unless to look at photos. A few days later though, Mrs. Zycinski—an oul yap, if ever there was one—took me to one of them cafes. Not my idea of a cafe, I have to say—chock full of computers. She wanted to show me what Mrs. Soyfer had found, so I humoured her just.

The cafe she knew was stowed-out—hardly surprising on a Saturday afternoon, and it bucketing. Coming down in stair rods, it was. She was nearly going to drag us the full length of the town to another place. Suddenly though—Praise the Lord—she spotted a phone box. One of them new modern ones. We must've looked a picture: two of us in our plastic macs, our brollies dripping, looking at a computer in a wee narrow phone box while, outside, the heavens emptied. Ye have to hand it to them though—Mrs. Soyfer & Mrs. Zycinski. Two of them were right in what they were saying. Page after page there was of hits—as Mrs. Zycinski called them too. Page after page about the frail wee woman who used to live across from me. A woman you'd hardly notice.

We even got a photo up of her.

The only disappointing thing was: the stuff was all in German. The vast majority of it anyhow. All credit to Ruth Zycinski though: when Mrs. Soyfer printed the stuff, she got out her dictionaries and started to work it all out. Even if ye don't know how they join up, the words themselves give ye an idea sure, sometimes, of what it is they're saying.

Mrs. Zycinski, God love her, had done the most of the work, apparently, before her daughter showed her the "Translate this page" thing.

Turns out she's been winning prizes, awards, distinctions—Mrs. Goodman. In Austria and Germany, mainly. Some of the highest honours going, we're talking about! The word *exile* kept coming up in what people were saying about her. The word *resistance* and all. Took me aback alright. Resistance, I thought, was something you only got in France just. Looking at it selfishly, the most exciting thing for me is: there's a girl working on a book. A lecturer by the name of Aisling Orr. *Forthcoming*, it is, according to what they call her "webpage." It's been forthcoming for a while. She wants to get her skates on. Ten years she's been at it, and she's still not bloody finished.

I wish to God the book was out. Brilliant, it would be. A *bilingual, critical edition of the poems of Vera Goodman* is how it's advertised. *Bilingual* means it'll be in German *and* English, thank God. Up shit creek we'd be, otherwise. *After the Flames* it's going to be called. That's what the working title is, anyhow.

Critical—I hope your woman Orr isn't too critical. Doesn't over-do it. You wouldn't want her spoiling the bloody thing, taking the good out of it.

I hope, above all, Mrs. Goodman lives to see it.

From what we can gather, there are poems about the war in there. Not the blitz side of things, but the camps. The death camps them poor craiturs—mere slips of men and women, not a pick on them—wasted away to nothing in. H-Block was nothing against them places, I always say. Most of the poems were written in the fifties and sixties—once her twins and their wee brother were of school age, probably, and the woman had the day to herself. What gets me is the thought of her sitting there—day in, day out—writing that stuff. Minding it all, then putting it down on paper. Ten minutes of any of them programmes on TV, sure, and I'm ready to slit my throat. Worse than Northern Ireland it is. And you wouldn't get me writing about that.

The poetry of the stayed-aways is what 'Translate this page' called it. *Of those that didn't come back.*

My heart's scalded, just thinking about it. Her here, in England.

Writing about that. In German too. Her own language. I chose to come to England, me. And at least the English speak English. Whereas—Mrs. Robertson, it was, round the corner from me, who cottoned on—if the three Goodman boys don't speak the lingo, they won't have read their mother's poems, will they? And her whatever age she is meanwhile, and them grown men now. Same goes for their wives and children, whoever sees them. And there's Vera Goodman, decades after it happened, torturing herself, writing it all down.

You have to hand it to Charlotte Soyfer: there's no stopping her. All ye ever hear is: she's been back on that there Internet. Unbeknownst to us, it turns out, Mrs. Goodman's been gallivanting. Doing personal appearances. Readings, interviews, festivals—thon kinda thing. Mrs. Soyfer's got all the details. Vienna, if you don't mind. Salzburg. Innsbruck. Klagenfurt—where she grew up—too. What must that have felt like? Places in Germany and all. And we hadn't noticed she was gone! Then there's the seminars they're doing, at universities all over the place. Conferences, too, where academics, experts—always the same names, it is—give talks on her. Imagine: some professor could turn up on *Mastermind* some week with that as his specialist subject: "The Life and Work of Vera Goodman"— and her across the road from me till recently there!

The Aisling Orr one, it turns out, has been giving talks too. She gives them in German, whatever the point of that is. All over the world she's been. Further than Mrs. Goodman even. She talked about her in Japan even. Funny that: the one talking about the poems getting more out of it than the one that bloody writes them.

Your woman Orr has spoken in Ireland too, Mrs. Soyfer said— which I was glad to hear. The North, especially, needs it.

The graduation was in July, there. No time, hardly, passed before we saw the proof. Wasn't that we didn't believe her, of course, but it was nice to see it confirmed just the same: the university's vice-chancellor had conferred upon Vera Goodman the degree of Doctor of Letters.

Ruth Zycinski, it was, who found out how it works. A friend of hers' grandson is doing a PhD, and according to him, you're nominated, ye don't actually study for one, and if they examine your case and it's strong enough, you're awarded one. Well, fair play to Vera Goodman, I say. All credit to her. The woman must've done something to deserve it cos them boys wouldn't be giving it to a wee woman lik her otherwise.

There was some craic, needless to say, the first time after that that *Dr.* Goodman boarded the bus home. Five or six of us there must've been, chatting up the back. I hope it wasn't too obvious. We were spread out, I suppose. Was the stop outside Marks she got on. We were dying to hear all her bars, of course.

'No, allow me!' Mrs. Soyfer whispered. 'Let me go down. I'll tell you everything later.'

She was right enough, of course: was only her was supposed to know. And it would only have terrified the poor woman if the whole bloody six of us had descended on her.

Have to admit: it was murder looking on. We could hardly hear a word, sure—with all the other conversations round about and the noise and rattle of the bus. Ye could see Charlotte Soyfer lapping it all up though, after shaking the woman's hand and congratulating her and making a wee joke about having to call her "Dr. Goodman" now. Ye could just imagine her saying 'Aw, that's lovely!' or 'Did she? Did they?' as she took it all in. Even with the full length of the bus between us though, I knew something was up. Something was wrong—I could see it. Could see Charlotte Soyfer looking wild serious as Mrs. Goodman told her.

It was tea and coffee at Mrs. Soyfer's thon day—whether she liked it or not.

'You'll come along too, won't you, Mrs. McCrossan?' she asked.

She meant it kindly enough. For me though, it was reminding me it wasn't automatic. The posh refugees could expect an invite. Oh aye. Not me, though. Not the Irish washerwoman who also came to England. All in the same boat back then, we were. Except we weren't. I didn't move in the circles in Belfast that they did, back in their own countries.

Bloody heart attack Mrs. Goodman would've had if she'd seen us all bundling off and piling into Charlotte Soyfer's, desperate to hear her business. Charlotte (as she is to some of them) regaled us all with the details. Only after we'd admired her carpet though—which is lovely down.

The graduation had been an *experience*. Everything Mrs. Goodman had expected, and more. Everything we'd expected. They gave her a posh hotel. A limo came to fetch her. She'd known Aisling's translations were good, she said, but realised even more when, read down a mic, they filled the beautiful hall. Her big moment came and she'd to stand up and step forward—and no, she didn't have to speak: just listen to what the Dean of the Faculty had to say about her. Was all straight out of Aisling's recent article about her, apparently. The Dean just stood there, reading it all out like she herself wrote it. At one point, seemingly, the vice-chancellor leaned forward and whispered that Vera could sit down. Suppose the boy was afraid of what all the excitement could do to her. That she wasn't strong enough. She was though. Told him so and all, did our Vera. Tired or not, she was determined to do things right. To enjoy her laureation.

At this point, Charlotte stopped and looked round the table, like that was her finished. She wasn't bloody on though. We hadn't come for this. Don't get me wrong: we wanted to hear that *too*. Lovely, it was. Every single word of it. And good luck to the woman. She deserved every bit. I wasn't the only one on the bus who'd noticed something strange though. That it wasn't all sweetness and light, what she had to tell.

'So what else happened?' Mrs. Zycinski blurted out.

If anyone had a right to know, she had—after all the translating she'd done.

'What do you mean: what else?' Mrs. Soyfer asked.

'We could see on the bus something was up.'

Charlotte Soyfer looked trapped. Had hoped to get away with

just the nice bits.

'Promise me you'll keep this to yourselves,' she pleaded.

We nodded.

'The person who nominated her has resigned,' she went on.

She must've seen the conclusion we jumped to.

'No, it wasn't over Mrs. Goodman! Her nomination had gone through—No, it was *in protest at the culture* she was *increasingly having to work within.*'

A couple of the ladies looked at each other as if to say*:* If that's all's eating her!

'The university could *refocus its academic activity*, if it wished,' Mrs. Soyfer continued—still quoting your woman obviously, or what Mrs. Goodman remembered of it. 'No way could she *implement a vision,* however, that she didn't share. What kind of a phrase was that, in any case? *Implement*? A *vision*?'

'Basically, Aisling Orr had handed in her notice. Mrs. Goodman had known before she travelled, of course. What neither of them anticipated, however, was it becoming an issue at dinner. The evening before, the ancient, wheelchair-bound old professor emeritus, not that he'd any right, demanded to know whether Goodman had known of Orr's intentions. That's how he referred to them: Goodman! Orr! Worse still, egged on by colleagues, he'd spoken across Vera and others—brass neck or what?—to quiz Dr. Orr. Not that the lady was having it. Short shrift, he got. To cut a long story short: they talked over dinner about nothing but internal politics. Not about Vera Goodman and her work. And there the poor soul had been dreading what they might ask. About poetics, say. Or worse still, the current situation in Iraq.'

Charlotte paused again. You could see she knew that last bit had lost people.

'I'm merely repeating what the woman said,' she said.

Time was getting on anyhow. The ladies with husbands still living started to make their excuses. Me, I was thinking about Mrs. Goodman. About someone across the way from me writing poetry.

Someone that close involved in resistance.

Your woman Orr and all. Best of jobs. Able to walk away from it though. Determined to.

What I want to know is: what's in them poems?

I'm desperate to talk to the woman.

Maybe once the translations come out, I'll be able to.

dachau-derry-knock
September 1979

For Karola and Rolf

University would be starting back soon & Liam was thinking about squeezing in one last trip. It had been a long, packed summer but, his first working abroad, & part of him didn't feel like going to Ireland. Not so soon after his long journey home anyhow. An' certainly not so soon after Mountbatten being killed & Warrenpoint. Aye, the Troubles were *bad* again getting.

When he said to his da, Big Liam pleaded with him:

'I know it wasn't for definite. I know you said you *might* just. Your granny's got her heart set on it but. She'll be wild disappointed if ye don't.'

Turned out: he could get a flight. From Glasgow too! An uncle said he'd collect him.

Soon as it was definite, it was Pope-this, Pope-that. Folk wouldn't shut up about it. The Pope would be in Ireland when Liam was. Maybe his gran & Bernie would take him? It would be a great opportunity if they did. *An honour.* Wasn't just the fact it was the first Polish Pope. Was the fact it was the centenary also: of the apparitions at Knock. 'You'll be representing us if you do go,' his da, strangely solemn, stressed. 'Jays—I hope he comes to Scotland one day too!'

His uncle Dermot picked him up. Liam. Not the Pope.

In the car back from Belfast, Dermot was desperate for bars. Liam felt awkward, not having any.

'How's yir da?' Dermot said, to prod him.

Liam wished he knew, wished he'd summit to say. It was hard to talk about Dad but.

'And yir mammy?'

'Same as ever.'

'And the weans? Not that you're weans any more! Age are ye now, youngfella?'

'Eighteen there—'

'Which makes the girls seventeen, sixteen—'

'Aye—'

'Any boyfriends yet?'

'Not that we know about,' said Liam.

He kept *stumm* about the German girl *he*'d met. 'How are things wi yous?' he asked instead.

'Jumpin!' said Dermot. 'Lookin forward to the Holy Father, we are.'

'Ye goin?'

'To Galway, aye. The Youth Mass. I'm going down wi the young ones. Are you?'

'My da was saying my Gran 'n' Bernie might take me.'

'What, to Knock?'

'Aye.'

'Do they know that?'

'Don't know.'

'I'd take ye to Galway only the bus is full.'

There was a silence that felt kinda awkward.

'I've never been to Knock,' Liam said, to break it. Not that he'd ever been to Galway.

'Have ye not?' Dermot sounded amazed. 'Your Granda O'Donnell, God rest him, loved Knock.'

They arrived. His gran saw them coming down the path. She'd still her seat by the fire that she looked up the garden to the street from. Even watching the news she kept an eye out, shifting onto her hip to try & get comfortable.

The key was in the door so Dermot turned it—to get the usual welcome from Shep. The living-room door—as ever—was wide open.

'Yes, Liam!' the ones in chorused. 'Welcome home!'

Nine years the O'Donnells were over in Scotland. Derry was still called *home* but.

His gran—in her favourite pinny—got up to hug him.

'It's good to see you, Liam, son.'

The 'How's yir daddy? How's yir mammy? How's the rest of the weans?' routine followed. The 'How long are yis over in Scotland?' one too. And of course: 'Would yis never think of coming back?'

Liam kept his counsel on that one.

'Maybe one day,' he lied.

One day, if he had his way, he'd marry & settle in Germany.

'Can I phone to say I landed?' he asked once things calmed down.

'Go ahead, son, aye!'

Liam headed out to the hall, shut the door behind him.

When he dialled the number, his mum answered.

'So are ye goin?' She sounded all excited.

'I don't know. No one's said. Dermot sounded surprised but when I mentioned it—'

'Put your gran on!' his mum said. 'I'll get your dad. You can't miss out on that!'

'Dad wants you, Gran,' Liam called over as he made his way back in.

His gran was on for a good while before she came back. Then others went racing out to speak to his da.

'Who's paying for this call?' was all they got out of Gran. 'Mind I'm paying when yis are quite finished!'

They were taking him to Knock! There might be a problem wi the B&B since he wasn't booked in; he could go wi them in the car but.

'Yir aunt Bernie & aunt Ita'll be sleepin in the car anyhow,' Gran said, 'so if the worst comes to the worst, ye can join them.'

Liam wasn't sure he fancied that.

'The actual Mass is on Sunday at the shrine,' his gran went on.

'We'll go down on Saturday but 'n' come back up on Monday.'

Ye could tell it couldn't come quick enough for her.

On the Saturday morning, the TV was already on when Liam went down for his breakfast.

'We can watch Phoenix Park before we go!' his gran, realising, said.

Over a million people were goney be there—most of them there already, it looked lik. The camera focused on the giant cross backed by sixty banners. Sixty foot high they were.

Looking at the crowd in Dublin, Liam was minded of *The Tin Drum*, the film he'd seen in Germany. About a boy, Oscar, it was, who at the age of three decided to stop growing; to toddle around wi his drum just. There was this great scene where he hid beneath a stage Hitler was on—and here, the crowd picked up on his beat & started waltzing!

Liam tried to tell Bernie, his gran interrupted but. 'What are ye tellin us that for? Are ye watchin this or not? It's once in a lifetime, mind!'

Stung, Liam forced himself to watch. It was a gorgeous morning, the commentator commented, and the *St. Patrick* was on time. Soon, ye saw the Air Corps meeting it, to escort the Pope as he landed. They came in over Killiney & flew up the Liffey, over all the bridges. The Pope must've seen them all in the Park. Cat was out of the bag if it was meant to be a secret.

Finally, the plane landed & the Pope kissed Irish soil.

'Hope there isni any dogs about!' Liam nearly joked nearly.

In his own house, he would've. Not here but. He minded last year, sure, when John Paul I died: folk stressing how only Paddy could get away wi *that*—his joke about the difference between the Pope & a Rowntrees Fruit Gum. Gran & all her oul buddies had been in stitches. No one was in any doubt but: anyone other than Paddy would be shown the door.

A wee girl of nine presented the Pope wi flowers.

He was walking in the footsteps of St. Patrick, John Paul said.

'Wasn't that wild nice of him,' Gran commented, 'saying that.'

Next, all eyes were on the helicopter—red, for some reason—that would take the Pope to the Park. The over-a-million had to be in there now.

The Mass itself dragged on. Nine cardinals, a hundred bishops, & any number of priests were *concelebrating* it (the stress went on the *con-*). The Pope gave his sermon, which people interpreted. John Paul didn't say as much, still wasn't having contraception but. Abortion & divorce were no-no's 'n' all.

Two thousand priests gave out Communion & soon it was time for the popemobile. "He's Got The Whole World In His Hands," folk were suddenly singing.

Swaying in unison they were. As if wee Oscar—a fellow Pole—was in among them, beating away at his drum.

The Pope was flying on to Drogheda. The three of them—Gran, Bernie, Liam—set off from Gran's house. Ita, they'd promised to collect.

'It's a pity we have to miss any coverage!' Gran was saying. 'A pity, in fact, Armagh was cancelled. A lot nearer it would've been—'

'We can listen to the wireless sure, Mammy!' Bernie said. 'It's not as if ye'll miss anything!'

It was the first Liam had heard of Armagh. 'Why was it cancelled?' he asked.

'Did ye not hear about Lord Mountbatten?'

Alles klar, he thought.

'Drogheda's the nearest the Pope'll get to the North,' his gran explained, leaving Liam half-wishing they were going *there*. It would be more symbolic. When Bernie said about loyalist paramilitaries but—the *very real fear* there'd be an attack—he changed his mind.

'D'ye need the toilet before we go?' Bernie asked. 'Cos no way am I stopping!'

Way she asked, Liam didn't know did she want him coming or

was he only getting cos Gran said.

Gran, fortunately, had an answer for her. 'Ye'll stop surely at some point, weegirl? In fact, ye'll stop when I tell ye!'

'I meant early on, Mother!' Bernie clarified.

They picked up Ita—who was all smiles as she joined Liam in the back—then headed for the Carlisle roundabout.

Before they were over the bridge even, Ita was asking how long they'd be?

'To Knock? Could be three or even four hours maybe!' Bernie said. 'God only knows, wi all the traffic!'

Three or four hours was long enough, Liam reckoned. If nowt compared to his thirty back from Munich.

The signposts, at first, were for Omagh & Strabane. Places where his mum had connections. After Strabane, they headed for Lifford— another place he'd heard of. It was just before Lifford ye crossed the border.

The soldiers must've been scunnered, right enough. Sick to the back teeth of papal colours. *Céad Mile Failte*: if they didn't know what it meant before, boy, they did so now.

A black boy hardly looked at them before he waved them through.

'And there was me thinkin the buggers would hold us up,' Ita said. 'That it would be just lik them to delay us—'

Liam, feeling nervous, changed the subject.

'This time last year I was in Berlin—an' I visited Checkpoint Charlie, Ita!'

'Did ye? What was that lik?'

'A bit disappointing, to be honest. The checkpoints here are scarier.'

'You're just back from Germany, aren't ye?'

'Yeah—'

'Any girlfriends?'

Liam blushed.

'That mean there *is*? I think he's got a *Fräulein*, Mother! Have ye?

A German sweetheart?'

Liam revealed nothing. Told them about Dachau instead. About getting a lift to Munich, a train back. About the hour's quick march through the mountains—pitch dark, trees either side—to get back to where he was working.

'Ye wouldn't catch me doing that!' Ita said wi a shudder.

Psycho was on, he explained, & they were all planning to watch it. That had been the reason for the rush.

He'd made it alright. Had even caught the end of what was on before.

'And wha' d'ye think it was about?'

Ita wasn't for guessing.

'H-block!' Liam told her. 'The dirty protest.'

'Was it really?'

'Yeah. And it was weird seeing the two things within hours of each other. Dachau. And then H-Block on the telly—'

'I suppose it would be, aye.'

The wireless was playing & replaying the highlights of Phoenix Park. The bits about the Irish people's faith. Their loyalty. The warning not to rest on past glories. The dangers of materialism. And affluence.

'What's affluence when it's at home anyway?' Bernie asked.

Liam hated that kinda question. Ita, fortunately, who was doing evening classes, was able to answer.

Over 'n' over again, the radio played the crowd singing. Ita & his gran sang along. Oscar would've been proud of them.

'Join in, youngfella!' Ita would give it, nudging Liam. Liam but wouldn't but, was too shy.

The Drogheda coverage followed. The nearest John Paul will get to the North, the commentator constantly reminded you. He'd be asking the IRA to give up violence, it was rumoured.

'Quite right 'n' all!' Gran said. 'And I hope they buckin listen!'

'Can't see it myself,' Ita answered.

Gran turned on her. 'Do ye want peace or not, daughter dear?'

'I do, aye.'

Was as if but Gran hadn't heard her: 'Ten years we've had of this! More than that! What the hell d'ye want? Another ten?'

'Course I don't!'

'Well buckin start praying then! Stead of sitting there saying ye can't see it!'

There was an atmosphere until Mass began & Gran started praying.

Then came the homily, the bit they were waiting for:

I wish to speak to all men and women engaged in violence.

Liam clocked the fact women were mentioned.

I appeal to you, in language of passionate pleading—

That was a Polish expression. Had to be.

On my knees I beg you to turn away from the paths of violence and to return to the ways of peace.

'Isn't that fair enough, the way he put it?' Gran commented. 'How could the boys object to that, ay?'

A quarter of a million people, many from the North, were there to hear it. There were no boos but. Nor was there any mention of people walking out.

Those who resort to violence always claim that only violence brings about change. You must know there is a political, peaceful way to justice—

'He's right enough!' Ita commented. 'What do you think, Bernie?'

'I'm too busy driving, me, to think!' Bernie said.

Browned off, she sounded.

The signs were for Sligo now.

They'd been passing through the likes of Killygordon. Ballybofey. Ballintra & Ballyshannon. Names Liam knew from his mother & father talking. Names ye kinda remembered whether ye'd been there or not.

Once they hit Sligo, they took a pit stop. Bernie pulled up behind a hotel.

The place they knew was across the bridge.

Bernie walked wi Liam. Out from behind the wheel, she was more friendly.

'Any other day, we'd be two-thirds of the way there now,' she told him. 'Don't be sayin to yir Granny; God knows what the roads'll be lik but, the closer we get to Knock.'

His gran looked tired, a bit, as they sat drinking their cuppas. 'Ma stays are killin me!' she said, wriggling to try to get comfortable.

Ita & Bernie were beginning to tire 'n' all.

'That's a lovely cuppa tay!' Ita commented. For once but, the others weren't for saying much.

Galway, they were heading for next.

'But don't worry, Liam—we turn off for Knock before that!' Bernie said.

The place-names here meant nothing to him. Charlestown was the first to ring any kind of bell.

Thankfully, it was fifteen miles or so only to Knock now.

'Aye, 'n' it could be the fifteen slowest!' Bernie warned.

'The Pope must be knackered, God love him!' Gran said. She suddenly just came out wi it. Liam nearly choked.

'What's *he* up to tonight?' Ita asked.

Way she said it, ye'd've thought he'd be out galavanting.

'The ones from the other churches it is first,' Gran answered. 'Then he's meeting the Taoiseach 'n' all the Cabinet.'

Ita winked at Liam. 'Listen to her! Your granny has it all memorised. Isn't she terrific for a woman in her seventies?'

By the time they got to the B&B, it was dark. They were able to park in its grounds. Bernie went to the door to speak to the woman.

'She's only a blow-up mattress to offer Liam,' she told them when she came back.

'That's okay, sure!' his gran piped up. 'It's only for tonight 'n' to-morrow!'

'She'll be wantin money for it—'

'Talk about buckin lousy!' his gran gave off. 'He'll have to give it to her, I suppose but! Tell her fine. Alright then.'

***

The next morning, Ita & Bernie were allowed in for breakfast. It was far from the full Irish. Again there was a charge but.

'She's chargin ye that for a cuppa tay 'n' toast? Yis have more money than sense!' Gran complained. 'I'd've waited, me!'

The wireless was on in the dining area & the previous day's highlights kept being repeated. Footsteps of St. Patrick. "The Whole World In His Hands." The Irish people's loyalty to their faith. Also, needless to say, John Paul pleading in passionate language to turn away from violence.

Liam nipped to the toilet. The night before, the presenter was saying, journalists, the world media, inspired by John Paul, had suddenly burst into song. "For He's a Jolly Good Fellow," they'd sung. Liam had to grin: ye had to hand it to Oscar & his drum! Some bloody nerve, the weeboy had.

The others filled him in when he got back.

Ita: 'Ye missed the bit about him meeting the other churches, Liam. It went well enough, cept: he'd wanted to meet them standing up but was tired 'n' had to sit down.'

Bernie: 'The Taoiseach gave him a statue of St. Patrick!'

Gran: 'He was up at the crack of dawn this morning to meet all the wee handicapped children! He's also met some Polish people. So it's next stop Clonmacnoise now, 'n' then onto Galway before Knock.'

'Listen to her!' Ita said again. 'Ye'd think ye were his personal secretary, Mother!'

The question was: would they try to drive to the shrine?

The B&B woman said they'd be better off walkin.

'I don't mind *now*. It's the gettin back afterwards!' Gran complained.

/ 170

Bernie decided to give it a go.

They'd hardly set off when they heard what awaited them: ten thousand cars descending on Knock.

There was no turning back & progress—even at that hour—was slow.

Bernie eventually conceded defeat & parked in someone's garden. 'It cost me an arm 'n' a leg!' she complained. 'They're buckin at it!'

'That's the Free Staters for you!' his gran said just. 'What do I always say? I swear to God—'n' this time I mean it: I'm never coming back!'

It had to be said: the Free Staters were making a mint. A hundred thousand welcomes, their arses. They were out to fleece ye! The B&B they were in was a brand-new bungalow & it was no bloody wonder, the prices they were chargin. Houses selling Cup-a-Soup had the cheek to charge a pound for it & every garden or field was a temporary car park. As for flags, posters, pennants, & the lik: it only had to have the Pope on it or CÉAD MILE FAILTE & they were charging through the nose for it.

'Themmins have me cursing so much, I'll need to go to confession!' Gran said.

When they finally got to the shrine, his gran pointed out the new basilica.

'We'll maybe take ye tomorrow, Liam. Right now but, we need to find a spot.'

The Mass might've been hours away, the place was filling up but.

They chose their spot. A woman nearby had a wireless. The Pope was done in Clonmacnoise, she reported. He'd praised the early missions & was due to land in Galway any minute. There'd be live coverage from the Ballybrit racecourse where two hundred thousand were waiting for him.

That was in Galway. Even in Knock, ones were afraid to move in case they lost their place. Normally, they'd do the Stations of the

Cross, perform the Fifteen Mysteries, Ita explained. Not today but.

The Youth Mass in Galway was broadcast in full. Those wi radios or within earshot ye could hear praying along. His gran & Bernie & Ita were saying all the responses. Sometimes Ita winked as if she was having him on.

The latest homily started & Liam tried to listen. The Pope believed in the youth of Ireland, he said. He loved them. The crowd in Galway went crazy. Soon "The Whole Wor-ld In His Hands" was being sung yet again. Jaysus, Oscar, gizza break! A joke's a joke, weeboy.

It was as if they'd sung too soon but. Next, it was religious and moral traditions the Pope was on about. The very soul of Ireland. He mentioned warped consciences. Rhymed off a list starting wi drugs, sex, drink. It was hard to imagine the youth fancying this much. One remark it took but just, for all of that to evaporate:

Young people of Ireland, I love you!

The crowd went wild.

The wireless couldn't get enough of it.

An' it wasn't wee Oscar's doing this time.

Galway went on so long, the Pope was late for Knock.

People stood & stood & waited & waited in the grey & damp.

'It's Bishop bloody Casey's fault!' someone gave it.

'They seem to've conveniently forgot Knock's the reason he came—'

'I've been here since midnight, me!'

'It's them poor invalids down at the basilica I feel sorry for—'

Folk, Liam noticed, were eating fish 'n' chips. His gran spotted them too.

'Them fish 'n' chips look gorgeous, Ita. Gaun ask the people where they bought them! I've not eaten since breakfast!'

When Ita found out, she was sent for some.

The Pope, needless to say, arrived before she got back & it was like a sin on Ita's soul, missing the start of Mass.

'I know *I* sent her,' Gran said. 'She shoulda made sure to get back but!'

If there was one thing you never were, it was late for Mass.

Gloomier & gloomier, it had been getting. Now it started to drizzle. Their one consolation was: the chips would warm them up.

Ita arrived back in time for the sermon. To hear JP2 stressing Knock was the goal of his journey. The chips were so hot they burned their mouths off. They still tucked in but, half-catching—if that—the words they'd come to hear.

They weren't the only ones only half-paying attention, Liam noticed. It had been too long a day.

'What d'ye mean I won't have fasted an hour before Communion?' a woman's husband snapped at her. 'I've been fastin all bloody day!'

It was lik: everyone's chips all froze between the bags & their lips somewhere.

'Your husband's right, missus!' an older man said. 'This Mass shoulda been over long before it started even. Wi the best will in the world, they can't expect us to fast all that time. Not when it's their faults—'

They all started scoffing their chips again.

An' when Communion was distributed, they all just received.

Eventually, the Mass was ended. They didn't go in peace but. The Pope had still to go round, sure, in his popemobile. Ye could see the roof working its way, the bubble underneath. 'This is history,' a man kept repeating, 'and we are here!'

Desperate, the O'Donnells were, for the Pope to reach where they were. Others kept delaying him but. "The Whole Wor-ld In His Hands:" Oscar, whoever seen him, was giving it laldy.

The Pope eventually got the closest he would get. It should've felt holy. Really holy. It was an anticlimax but. Pope or no Pope, he was late. The boy had kept them waiting. And now all ye saw of him was this.

To make things worse: the tour was cut short. Cos night was falling.

'We're the lucky ones,' Gran kept saying. 'There's parts of the crowd he didn't get anywhere near.'

Even she sounded wild let-down but.

***

Another morning, another breakfast.

Ita & Bernie popped in again.

'Yis'll never learn, will yis?' their mother said. 'I wouldn't give them the buckin money!'

The highlights were being repeated still & the Pope's final day was being discussed. For the ones at the O'Donnell table but, it was as if it was over already.

Gran was still harping on about the day before's delays. The schedule should've been kept to. Bishop buckin Casey should've seen to it.

'Here, I forgot to tell yis yesterday, wi all the excitement!' Ita was suddenly saying. 'Mind I went away for fish 'n' chips? Well, at one point a Belfast woman I was speakin to overheard a wee local woman sayin the Pope had been held up. Wild shook up, your woman from Belfast was. O Jesus, Mary 'n' Saint Joseph! she said, blissin herself. The woman from Knock looked at her just. It's not that bad, love, she said. He's just a bit delayed. Next thing, your woman from Belfast's blissin herself again. O thanks be to God, missus, says she. When you said he was held up, I thought the paramilitaries had got him!'

They all laughed. Gran got Ita to repeat it even, for the B&B woman.

'Where's the Pope today, Mother, anyway?' Ita pretended to ask. Ye could hear it was just for the sake of it. Gran could probably tell even.

She rhymed the answer off anyhow: 'Maynooth, Limerick, Shannon Airport, it is. An' then on to America.'

'Rather him than me!' Ita said. 'Don't know about yous—for me right now but, Derry's far enough!'

Not even *Young people of Ireland*—the endless repeats & all the cheering & singing—was managing to gee them up. They were all just sitting there, shattered.

'Would ye say that rain's actually raining?' Ita—looking out—asked. 'Or is it just threatening just?'

'No, that's it on,' Bernie answered.

'Wouldn't it be great if we did get peace?' Gran piped up. 'If the Pope's visit did bring it about? That's all I wish for now. I'd go to my grave happy even, if I thought he'd brought peace.'

It was agreed they'd go to the shrine before they headed home.

The rain, miraculously, had gone off again.

It wasn't just Mary just, a century before, Liam now learned. Joseph & John the Evangelist had accompanied her.

'A hundred years ago this year,' his gran stressed. 'Imagine!'

'Mind now 'n' say a wee prayer for your Granda Donnell, Liam,' Ita whispered. 'He'd a great devotion to Knock. Raised a lot of money for Monsignor Horan.'

They got to where the Mass was held to find you could walk on the altar.

Could even stand on the very spot where John Paul had stood.

Unusual thing was: no one had thought to charge for it.

The carpet was indigo-ey blue.

The big cross was white.

You stood there & it was nearly as if the Pope hadn't been at all lik.

All that excitement already over.

Before they left, his gran showed Liam where the Blessed Virgin had appeared. Where the Pope had knelt to pray the day before.

You couldn't see nothing.

They squared up at the B&B & headed back to the border.

The coverage on the wireless was now onto Maynooth. Wee bloody Oscar had been at it again obviously: 'We want the Pope! We want the Pope!' young seminarians had chanted. The official music had no chance apparently. The chants & all the singing drownded it out.

This time, the Pope focused on priests breaking their vows. He'd a few words as well for ones not wearing their collars.

The O'Donnells listened to Limerick as they motored back to the North. The Pope's last address, here in Ireland. *Your country seems in a sense to be living again the temptations of Christ* was the quote picked up on this time.

DISCUSS, Liam thought. *1,000 words by Monday*. Well seein uni was starting back.

"Will Ye No Come Back Again," the crowd sang this time. And "Come Back to Éireann."

Ye had to hand it to wee Oscar: he'd fairly extended his repertoire! An' infiltrated the band while he was at it!

A long way from Derry the O'Donnells were still when the Pope boarded his flight from Shannon to Boston. The President & Cardinal O'Fiaich were seeing him off.

A news bulletin followed on the hour. The IRA had issued a statement.

At the first mention of *evil British presence,* Gran flipped: 'It's the same oul shite! Switch it off! I don't want to hear it!'

Force, the statement went on, was *by far* the only way to get rid of that presence.

'Turn it off, Bernie, I said!'

Once they'd succeeded, the IRA was claiming, the Church would have *no difficulty* in recognising them.

Gran had had enough: 'Trust themmins to spoil it all for everyone!'

She reached to switch the wireless off herself.

'Excommunication's too bloody good for them!'

Hearing her & seeing her, Liam wanted to say something. Or do something. Not that he knew exactly what. Ita, seeming to realise, shook her head.

'Naw, don't be saying nothing, Liam!' she whispered, across the back seat. 'You're better off leaving it, sure. Not saying nothing.'

a story when you

It's not often I come here, to *sih*. I'll stop for petrol, aye, at the supermarket starting with *tih,* will do the occasional food shop. Today, I'm here with my four-year-old godson in *curly kih, curly kih*—as the wee man has started calling it, now his sister's learning to read. The girls got to *sih* before us, are shopping for dinner at *tih*. When they're ready, they'll come and get us.

Curly kih curly kih's as far as I ever go here, *sih* doesn't interest me otherwise. It's surprisingly okay, though: this cafe that isn't; this sectioned-off space in the aisle.

Anyway: an espresso, a smoothie & a bag of mini muffins, and us two boys grab seats. Owen's straight into the muffins. I have the kind I like least. Leave one of each for his sister. Then, sure enough, it's cue the new routine:

Tell me a story when you were two, Alec.

The story that started it all. The *I-wet-myself-when-I-was-a-wee-boy-too* one.

'When I was two, I was learning to use the potty over on the newspapers. And one Friday night—it was bath-time, in front of the fire—your granda lifted me over his head, and he was tickling me and laughing out loud as I kicked my legs in the air. I'd no clothes on, of course. It ended up: he tickled me so much, he made me do a pee-pee, and he was laughing so much, the pee-pee went in his mouth!'

I ooh-yugh as the wee man's face lights up. He's heard the story loads of times, still laughs though like the first time.

We're off. He wants more:

Tell me a story when you were four.

'When I was four, I had a toy farm, and sometimes my granny, your nana's mum, would buy me new animals. One time though, the man in the shop gave her a dirty pig and a dirty sheep, in among the animals she bought, and I said no, I didn't want them—cos there was muck on the pig's belly, and mud on the wool of the sheep, and I wanted clean ones. Take them back, I told her. She made me go with her. The man took them and looked at them and said there was nothing wrong with them but he'd change them this time. I was a silly moo though, he said, as he gave me the new ones.'

Silly moo gets a laugh.

'Why'd he call you a silly moo, Alec?'

'Because it was natural, he said. Animals get dirty!'

Time for another.

Tell me a story when you were sixteen is next.

Then: *When you were forty* (he doesn't just do young ages, Owen).

Then: *Twenty-seven*—

Even a couple of weeks ago, he'd've said *four-oh, two-seven,* I realise.

When you were thirty-three is next—

And again, I've to do my sums, my year of birth plus thirty-three this time.

Then *nineteen*—

Uni. I try to remember where I was that summer, what I was doing that summer.

Then *forty-six*—

It's also case of finding a story I can tell a wee boy.

When you were twenty-three—

'When I was twenty-three, I was on holiday in Holland, and the outdoor swimming pool closed at six o'clock. If it was nice weather though, everyone just waited in the park till they saw the man driving home, the wee white van heading out the gate. Then we all broke in again, through holes in the fence in the bushes. And one time, I was climbing through, wearing new trousers, and all I heard was *r-r-r-r-i-i-i-p-p-p-p,* right down the leg! I'd never torn my trousers when I was wee, I tore them when I was twenty-three though!'

'Was Nana angry?'

The girls now appear, and sure enough: Owen asks Nana does she remember my good cords? The girls, it turns out, are heading off again. Rosie's to stay with us to do her reading.

As if. Not a hope. Soon, more like, they're both at it:

Tell me a story when you were (whatever), Alec—

Rosie's hoping to hit on something naughty, I can tell, whereas Owen, now on my knee, is fading. I know the feeling.

Tell me a story when you were seven (next-door's terrier eating our pet chickens).

When you were forty-two (Siobhan in Mummy's tummy).

Thirteen (the school trip to Millport).

Eighteen (thirty-three hours on the train and boat and another two trains to Austria. The Belgian guy wakening me, insisting on a seat).

Eleven.

'When I was eleven, I moved up to the big school and we started learning French. And the teacher would say *levez-vous* and we all had to stand up, then *asseyez vous,* and we all had to sit down again. Then: *comment vous appelez-vous?* she'd ask and I'd have to say *Je m'appelle Alec!*'

I'm struggling now. The bottom of the infamous barrel. Owen though is laughing, satisfied.

'You're easily pleased, kiddo,' my da would've said.

A woman behind us, older than me, and her mother (I would guess) start to make to leave. I spot the barricade of coats & shift to make some space.

'Can you manage there?'

The older woman laughs.

'I can, thank you, yes!' Then, with a wink: 'I could listen to your wee stories all day!'

Rosie and Owen laugh, delighted. Say bye-bye and the women set off.

Tell me a story when you were zehero! Owen now demands.

Zero's a new one. He thinks he's got me.

'When I was zero, I was in your Nana's tummy for nine months. When the nine months were up, that was me ready and she let me out. And wha' d'ye think? On the day I popped out, it was MY BIRTHDAY!'

He clocks my tone of voice, Owen, and laughs.

'Is that it?' he asks. 'Is that the story?'

'That's the story, pal!' I tell him, and him & his sister laugh.

beheading the virgin mary

'Twas the day after Xmas & they celebrated it that year by beheading the Blessed Virgin. Aye, that's what Boxing Day that year would be remembered for, probably. Fair enough, aye: it was Big Liam's last Xmas, God have mercy on him, the last time he'd his family all around him, family as in: all his grandweans 'n' all, an' mind: it was Annette's Fraser's first Xmas without his mother 'n' all, R.I.P, & the twins, barely out of nappies, God love them, were missing their Nana Sheila. Apart from them two things but, it was the same old same old, no doubt: the rafters ringing, decorations swaying, & balloons bobbing everywhere as the weans charged round the hall, the odd one or two maybe clinging to their dads, to begin wi anyway, while the O'Donnell sisters & one or two of the men, maybe, started getting the food going. Any money: wee Kelly'd made a beeline for her aunt Bernie & was getting her hair brushed: 'Ye look like ye've been dragged through a hedge backwards, weegirl!' Any money 'n' all: Keith M was up dad-dancing (not that him & Ciara have even got weans) & Sean arrived, lik every other year, wi his Boxing Day bargains he handed out—himself—as Xmas presents, naw, Annette, he wasn't prepared to wait for Santa to get there & the twins, bet ye, both sets, Orla's two girls as well as Annette & Fraser's boys, would've been taunting Bernie's Josh, the only only child & the toddlers in the family, whoever seen them, would've been traipsing round after their big cousins, idolising them though they very rarely seen them—their big cousins, needless to say, hating this attention & doing their damnedest to shake the wee ones off & they'd've got a total of eight words, maybe, out of Derek, Orla's husband, in all the time he was there, one of them the one *hi* that was supposed to do for everyone, not even a Merry bloody Xmas did ye get even & whether certain ones in the family had *shown* all year or not, Bridget, to keep the peace, would've been talking to everyone, Liam, God rest him, less so & the weans, the nursery-age ones especially, would've raced across the hall when young '*Liam!* LIAM! *Uncle* LIAM!' arrived, hurling themselves at him & leaping into his arms, the ones that didn't get lifted clinging to his legs, him—unable to see—trying not to tread on them, comforting, calming, assuring, the ones that had been too slow & the *sangwiches* (as Hamish called them) would all have had cheese in them, on one tray, and wafer-thin ham, on the other; pan, needless to say, all of them bloody pan & you'd've seen the ones that liked their food, that knew about food, sticking to the soup, the turnip & parsnip, or to Liam's lentils, then Ciara's fruit loaf to round things off, that or tiramisu & no doubt the priest who'd've come in when the food did & insisted on doing a blessing, would've tried his ecumenical best, 'I gather some of you are non-Catholic. Well, you're very welcome so you are' & Liam, not wanting to hurt his mother & father lik, might not've asked where that left the *not-anythings,* he'd've made some joke bet-ye-any-money but about being a *non-Protestant* himself & some of them would've laughed & some of them would've been looking to see was it okay to laugh, the sons-in-law in particular, one or two of them, would've maybe played it safe, settled just for a grin just, Big Liam but, not for the first time, would've noticed young Liam, not for the first time either, not calling Father "Father," not giving him his place lik, worse than him himself his eldest boy was when it came to the buckin clergy, allergic, aye that was the word: wild-wild *allergic* he was, they both were, to clergy; that non-Protestant line was hardly even a joke even, more lik a running battle, it was, poor Father having to fake a smile, having—year in year out—to take it. An' when Santa did finally arrive—after Father left—they couldn't give the presents out, sure, when they'd not got the priest nothing this year again—when Santa did arrive, the stupid big lump, bet ye, would still've had Hamish's polo top on, or Derek's fleece, under his coat—how bloody stupid can you get?—an' he'd have stocking fillers maybe, for the adults, freebies but they'd be, from hotel rooms lik, or corporate bits & pieces: mouse pads or whatever from themmins Fraser Thingmy works for, which was nearly as bad as Cahal's wife—talk about being tight!—buying to the other weans alright, the nieces & nephews, not but to the aunts & uncles who'd no weans of their own, whereas Sean's Marie could make the least wee thing look lovely. Thoughtful, lik.

All them things, granted, are things the family mind about that particular Boxing Day, about most recent Boxing Days since they started hiring a hall, what young Liam minds most but—apart from wee Kelly suddenly coughing up phlegm suddenly & his mother telling her just to cough it up just, *cough it all up, love, an' if it may be a row of houses*—is the ball, his nephews, two or three of them, having torn themselves away from the PS3 finally, kicking a ball around over beside the fire exit & his heart being in his mouth sometimes as one of the wee infants suddenly invaded the pitch, was suddenly crawling across it, in danger of being walloped or flattened or both & what was even worse lik: the other wee ones, oblivious to any danger, oblivious to the shouts of *Watch out &* their names being called, oblivious to the lucky ones being ushered away to safety, were *sure* to follow.

That's not what happened but.

Naw, no one was flattened, the ball didn't smack some poor wean in the face, naw: Baby God's mammy got it. Baby God's *mummy*, as the youngest wee grandweans—being Scotch—call her. What they say happened was: Cahal & Marie's second boy, Conor, back-heeled the ball to his big brother Jason & Jason tried to pass it, apparently, straight to Orla's Stuart, first touch lik, not stopping to control it first, the ball but banana-ed off his foot & while it didn't go round all the cushions exactly, it did hammer off the back wall & Holy God—even just thinking about it!—ricocheted—naw—*aye*! straight at the Virgin Mary, straight onto her chest. The Blessed Virgin's ball control was rotten but, seemingly, her first touch not up to scratch, not that their eyes were on the ball any more, Mary—

Good Mother of God!—was losing her head, sure, instant it was, lik in slow motion 'n' all but, as her head wobbled, toppled backwards & then—*aw Christ, naw*—took a tumble. Liam minds Bonetti the Cat, aka Sean, the nearest adult, diving to his right suddenly; he was a goalie, mind, years ago, school team, then the Juniors, nearly went professional the same boy, not, right enough, that that was helping him at this particular moment cos the head—that lovely face the Virgin Mary has 'n' all—was spinning just beyond his fingertips, just beyond his reach, the distance he was missing her by agonisingly short. As if the Blessed Virgin had been guillotined, it was, from the front or from the side but, not from above. Lik a clean cut anyhow, it was, as the body stayed put, the head but thudded to the floor. Okay, so the feared smithereens might not've happened, Stuart but was in instant tears though it wasn't him that kicked it & his tears panicked—totally panicked—the wee young ones, God love them, bedlam it was, pandemonium apparently, in floods of tears they were: first, rooted to the spot, their wee bodies tense as anything, their eyes locked on their wailing cousins, then: still, as they flung themselves into their mothers' & fathers' arms, *Baby-God's-mummy* this, *Baby-God's-mum* that being all ye bloody heard. PlayStation ban a cert nearly now or not, their big cousin, Jason, was struggling not to laugh & Sean: 'Don't worry, everyone,' he was soon announcing, 'I'll deal wi it. I'll speak to the priest!' An attempt to calm all the commotion, of course, not that he'd a hope of being heard lik, wi the screams of all the weans & the older boys protesting their innocence. He tried to make light, it seems, Sean, of what had happened: 'If the worst comes to the worst, we'll all chip in 'n' buy him a new one, sure. She was on her last legs, Mary, anyhow. On her way out, if you ask me.' Cahal backed him up, seemingly: 'Aye, you're right there, bruv. Sure the statue would still be in the chapel itself still otherwise.' 'It's embarrassing nevertheless,' Derek Mc-buckin-Sween, but, was heard to mutter, 'it still shouldn't have happened.' The bugger may've doubled his word count, Orla was in no way grateful but: 'Shut up, you!' she roared at him just, going off to get the priest. Then all ye heard was: 'It wisni me!' Choruses of it. 'It wisni me either!' 'Aye, well it definitely wasn't me!' & 'Did I say I was confiscating your PlayStation? Did I?' & 'Look, Granda, look! Look, Nana!' as Big Liam & Bridget finally made it through the throng. 'Jesus, Mary, & Saint Joseph, how did that happen? Which of yis done that?' Big Liam—seeing the damage—asked. A big softy he was, always, God rest his soul, when it came to the Blessed Virgin. He always did have a special devotion to her. The same can't be said of his second son, Sean. Fair enough, aye: he lifted Mary's head & sat it back on the statue. To show it would go, maybe. 'Nothing a taste of Super Glue wouldn't fix—or nail varnish,' he went on to joke but, before setting the head down on the cleanest dirty plate. 'For safekeeping,' he claimed, 'There's been enough damage already, sure.' The weans gathered round to look lik the day before they'd've gathered round the manger. 'What do ye think we'd get on eBay for her?' Sean whispered to Keith, seemingly. '*Second-hand Virgin—one previous owner*!' The weans who heard him sniggered, or were looking—their turn now—to see was it okay to find that funny? An immediate yellow card, it was, for Sean O'Donnell but. 'That's enough of that, you!' Annette warned him. 'Some of these uns have their First Communions to make this year.' Not that the caution worked lik. Worse than weans the O'Donnell brothers are when they start, sure. Cahal, it was, next. Maybe it was the last of the *sangwiches* that close to Mary's face, or the final scrapings of tiramisu that made him think it; suddenly but, he was asking Sean, 'D'ye think she looks famished, bruv—the Blessed Virgin?' Sean, apparently, walked straight into the trap. 'Naw,' the story goes, he said just. 'Aye, well she *will*,' said Cahal, laughing. 'Give it a couple of hours 'n' she *will*. Fact: her stomach's goney think her throat's been cut!'

Jason & Liam, meanwhile, had taken themselves off, seemingly—peeled themselves off from the group, young Liam having no doubt clocked that look Jason can sometimes give ye sometimes. All hell could be breaking loose & cool as a cucumber, he'll look at ye, the youngfella, as if to say 'A word, please?' & ye have to hand it to him: the same boy can speak some sense. Liam was letting on this time, but, to be annoyed. 'Some man you are, nephew! There you were yesterday, celebrating the birth of the Baby Jesus, visiting the crib, kissing the foot of the infant maybe even, & twenty-four hours later, not even, you're decapitating the poor wean's mother! Is that what you're trying to tell me?' Jason, but, was fit for him but & when Liam challenged him again, 'Is that what you're telling me?' the youngfella—twelve now—stood his ground: 'Yeah—yeah, it is,' he said, politely. 'That *is* what I'm telling you.'

Liam let on to cuff him one. High-fived him then instead.

'Respect, mucker!' he said. Then: 'Yo dude, that was sick to the max, man!' he was suddenly giving it next.

'Naw—*respect,* mucker!' Liam repeated, apparently, all serious again. 'Just don't go telling your granda I said that!'

'I wouldn't want to upset him, sure, at his age,' he explained, when Jason just looked at him just.

bonus material

the completely true story
of the goldfish ghost —

a children's book in search of an illustrator

Pour Alice et Justin

[1]

How it all started was: their daddy came home one night &
totally out of the blue announced they were going on holiday.

They'd never been on holiday.

To Malin Head, it was. And the next day.

[2]

Malin Head was the most northerly point in Ireland.

Their uncle Paddy & aunt Fiona went there every year.

They'd have to cross the border, so they'd have to.

'Most northerly point' meant: if you went any further, you'd
fall in.

'Is it far, Daddy?'

It was a wee bit far, aye. If they were good but, he'd buy them
sweets but. An' they'd know they were getting close cos there was
a bridge wi thirteen bumps on it.

[3]

The next day, they set off much later than their daddy had said.

Packing took forever and was very boring.

Sean nearly felt the back of his father's hand.

'Is that you finished?' their daddy said, when finally their
mammy was.

[4]

Soon, the five weans were across the back seat:

Liam, Ciara, Annette, Sean, Bernadette—

From the eldest (just turned six) to the youngest (just turned two).

There mustn't have been no sink where they were going.

Their mammy was packing *everything*—

The kitchen sink 'n' all, their daddy told them.

[5]

At the last minute, their mammy remembered the goldfish.

She came running out of the house, carrying the bowl wi a saucer over it.

'What?? Is the fish coming too??' their daddy asked.

'Naw, smartarse!' their mammy said. 'We'll need to stop at William St. but. I'll need to ask my mother to look after it!'

She'd been so busy thinking of everything else, she'd forgotten poor wee Shep.

'Here, you hold that, son!' she said, placing the bowl squarely on Liam's lap.

'I want to hold it!' Ciara & Annette chorused.

Their mammy still gave it to Liam but.

It was *his* fish.

[6]

Their Mammy Cluskey came out to the door when she heard the car pull up.

'Course I'll look after Shep!' she assured Liam.

She gave him a big big hug. He, after all, was her eldest grandchild.

'Good job you thought of it, Bridget!' she said to his mammy.

'Would've been belly-side up you'd've been coming back to, otherwise!'

[7]

They didn't cross the bridge.

They left Derry the other way.

[8]

When the border was coming up, their daddy minded them—again—to be on their *best* behaviour.

'Don't be lookin lik smugglers on me now!'

[9]

'We left the goldfish at Mammy Cluskey's, mister!' Annette blurted out when the very severe Customs man looked in her window.

[10]

After the border came MUFF and QUEEGLEY'S POINT.

Then the mountain you had to go over to get to CARDONAGH.

Finally—at long last—they reached the bumpy bridge.

Liam was just glad he hadn't still Shep on his knee.

The other weans loved the thirteen bumps.

'Do it again, Daddy!' they roared. 'Do it again!'

Their mammy wasn't worth tuppence, so she wasn't, as he reversed the car across.

Someone could've come racing round the bend, sure!

[11]

When they reached Malin Head, they went to their own wee farmhouse first.

It had a thatched roof & a well down the lane.

Then they went to say hello to Uncle Paddy & Aunt Fiona while it was still daylight.

[12]

The McCluskeys lived in a wee house made of corrugated iron.

'Corrugated' meant: lik all wee waves lik.

The house was next to the beach. Or *above* it, more lik.

You had to go down stones to get to the sand.

There was one steep hill of stones, then a wee sort of landing, then a not-so-steep hill of stones. Then you were on the sand.

[13]

In the evening, before the sun went down, the tide came in.

More than halfway up the top half of the stones, it was.

Any further & it would've flooded the grass Paddy & Fiona's house was on.

What was even scarier was looking down into it.

Seeing how deep it was. How it swoll & rose & slapped against the stones.

The noise was scary.

[14]

You could see the sea's belly & ye knew there was no way ye wanted to be in there, not wi a rubber ring even.

'Ye could drown and die!' their mammy warned them.

'An' don't come crying to me if ye do!' their daddy added. 'Cos ye'll get no sympathy!'

[15]

Liam thought he'd have nightmares that night. He didn't but.

He remembered Shep before he went to sleep.

An' what was the first thing he thought of in the morning?

Which just went to show what a good friend he was.

[16]

In the days that followed, any time they were at Fiona & Paddy's, Liam went wi his cousins to the rocks.

It was safe while the tide was out.

'Don't be forgetting your buckets 'n' spades & fishing nets now!' said Uncle Paddy.

The girls just stayed around the house just.

[17]

His cousins showed Liam the rock pools.

Hours & hours they spent, watching & catching sticklebacks & shrimps.

The sticklebacks weren't that big. You could catch loads but.

One day, there was a really big one. Liam, it was, who spotted it.

Wi all the excitement of it, Shep went out of his head.

[18]

When it came to going back to the house, the others were better at climbing.

His cousins were used to the stones, sure.

Liam ended up on his bum just.

Every time he tried to take a step, the stones would slip away & he'd slide back down them backwards.

Exhausting, it was. Heartbreaking.

[19]

One time, it was lik his legs got stuck & his daddy'd to come & carry him—even though he'd turned six.

[20]

Then one day, towards the end of the holiday, he was down at the beach on his own.

They still hadn't had no rain.

'There's people pays hundreds of pounds,' Paddy kept saying, 'to go to Spain for sunshine lik this!'

Liam was standing in the water when—he thought he wasn't seeing right!—a goldfish swam past.

[21]

Not daring to breathe, he crept forward, not wanting to scare it.

He managed to slip his bucket in without the fish noticing.

Next thing he knew, he'd caught it!

It was strange looking at a goldfish at the bottom of an orange bucket.

Specially when, normally, they went round and round in bowls!

The wriggles of it 'n' all! Was as if it was trying to tell him something!

Sometimes, when it was up against the plastic, you'd've thought the thing had vanished.

[22]

Liam was so pleased, he wanted to show the rest of them.

His new fish looked just lik Shep, his goldfish back in Derry.

Shep's spitting image, it was!

People would think they were twins, so they would!

[23]

He marched towards the house.

Crossing the sand was okay. In no time at all but, he'd to face the bloody stones.

The second lot looked even steeper even & slippier than usual.

Liam's heart sank.

He *knew* he wouldn't manage.

If he couldn't get up on his own, how was he going to do it wi a fish in a bucket of water?

[24]

He tried anyway.

The water was splashing everywhere each time he slipped.

He emptied some out so it wouldn't drown him.

Soon there was just a wee taste for the fish.

[25]

Liam tried & tried, wasn't getting anywhere but.

He tried freeing his hands.

He put the bucket down & took a few steps; then lifted the bucket up & placed it further up.

Was a case of always trying to climb to where the bucket was.

He just kept slipping—slipping & slipping—but.

[26]

He was terrified of the bucket toppling over.

Had visions of the bucket going flying & the poor wee fish landing on the stones. Of it flopping round, dying—lik the fish the men at the pier caught.

The thing was: if there was no water, the poor wee thing would die.

The opposite of drowning was what would happen.

[27]

He could see his uncle Paddy's & aunt Fiona's.

Today but of all days but, there was no one there to help.

The stones had won, so they had. Had beaten him.

Finally, reluctantly, he headed back down.

There was nothing else for it: he'd have to let it go, the new wee fish.

'It's back into the sea for you, boy!' he told it.

[28]

He allowed himself to hold it before he set it free.

He hadn't had it long, he loved it even so but.

A wee bit down, he was, as he watched the thing swim off.

[29]

This time, he managed.

On his hands & knees & wi a bit of effort, he made it up the stones.

Wi the bucket empty, it didn't matter what happened now, sure.

[30]

Soon as he seen her, he started to tell his mammy.

'I caught a goldfish, Mammy—'

In the middle of what he was saying, Aunt Fiona came in & he'd to start all over, so he had to.

A complete nuisance, it was. It kept happening but. In would come another person & his mammy would tell him to go back & start at the start.

'Gaun, son! Your uncle Paddy would enjoy it, sure!'

Liam thought he was never going to get to *The End*.

[31]

'You don't get goldfish in the sea, don't ye not?' Fiona said to Paddy when, finally, Liam did.

'Never mind, sure you'll see your own wee goldfish when we get back to Derry,' his mammy said.

[32]

As it happened, he didn't.

They got home to find his own wee goldfish was dead, God love it.

Shep had kicked the bucket a couple of days before.

His Mammy Cluskey was just in the door from ten Mass, she told them, when she spotted him: belly-side up.

Liam wanted to cry. He could see Mammy Cluskey was close to tears 'n' all but, so he didn't.

Him crying would only make her cry, sure.

[33]

His mammy hugged him & promised him a new fish.

Mammy Cluskey gave him some of her make-things-better swiddies.

It wasn't *their* fish that died, she gave the rest of them some 'n' all but.

The swiddies didn't taste as nice as usual.

There was something wrong wi his tastebuds maybe.

[34]

Before they left, Liam overheard Mammy Cluskey telling his daddy she'd flushed it down the toilet.

His daddy forced her to admit it.

Liam wasn't supposed to know—but now he knew but.

Down the toilet was where wee Shep went.

[35]

That's not where the story ends but.

Twelve years later, Liam was a student over in Scotland & one night, in the queue in the canteen, he got talking to two girls. Lovely looking, they were.

He started to tell them his goldfish story for some reason.

About the goldfish he found in the water at Malin Head.

Marine Biology they must've been doing.

[36]

Anyhow, it was all them years later, in that queue, talking to them two, that Liam realised the story was a *ghost* story.

That the goldfish at Malin Head had been his own wee goldfish.

That his dead fish had come to say goodbye.

[37]

'An' I've just realised, talking to you two ladies, that it's a ghost story, my goldfish story!' he told them. 'The fish I caught in my bucket must've been a ghost!'

'Shep, it was!' he explained, seeing the looks he was getting. 'He made his way to the Head to say goodbye!'

'Awww,' said the girl wi the blue eyes. 'That's dead nice!'

The red-haired girl must've agreed, so she must've, cos she leaned across & kissed Liam.

It was the totiest wee peck just.

But it felt lik what it would feel lik but if a goldfish kissed you.

the end

acknowledgements

'big trouble' and 'somewhere down the line' were written in response to commissions from the Scottish Arts Council (now Creative Scotland) and Glasgow Celtic FC, respectively. The former story appeared on the SAC website; the latter in the *Celtic View*. 'big trouble' was inspired, in part, by my time as a Hermann Kesten Fellow in Nuremberg—where we visited the Party Rally Grounds.

'enough to make your heart' was published in *Best European Fiction 2012* (Dalkey Archive, USA). Extracts were read at launches in Cork, Dublin, and Edinburgh.

The following were first published in literary magazines and journals:

'a recent death' in: *Causeway/Cabhsair* (Aberdeen)
'kenny ryan' in: *International Literary Quarterly* (online)
'the troubles (for you)' in: *Causeway/Cabhsair* (Aberdeen)
'dachau-derry-knock' in: *Gutter* 3 (Glasgow)
'a trip to carfin' in: *The Hudson Review* (New York)

I wish to thank all of the editors involved. Not least for their commitment to short stories.

'the way to a man's heart' is an Irish-Scottish version of a Russian-American story that Lara Vapnyar had yet to write when she first mentioned it to me. Lara's "Borscht" subsequently appeared in her collection *Broccoli and Other Tales of Food and Love* (Pantheon Books 2008). My own story—triggered by that initial conversation—was first drafted during a residency at the Writers' House in Szigliget (Hungary).

A number of these stories were first written, or revised, at Hotel Chevillon in Grez-sur-Loing (thanks to the Robert Louis Stevenson Memorial Award & subsequent invitations to the *Journées*

Stevenson); in the city of Berne (thanks to the sadly now defunct exchange with Glasgow); at Ledig House (in New York State); in the Monastère de Saorge (France); the apartment of the Slovene Writers' Association in Ljubljana; and at Hawthornden Castle (Edinburgh). My thanks to the wonderful people behind these retreats & exchanges.

David Kinloch, Catherine McInerney, Simon Biggam, Peter Schranz, Jean-Jacques Boin, Christilla Pelle-Douel, Gregor Podlogar & Barry Wallenstein deserve special mention here. Maggie Graham read early versions of the two most recent stories. My thanks also goes to Tess Lewis, for forwarding & creating crucial links. And, generally, to the good folks behind the Scottish and Irish Writers' Centres.

My translation work would not exist without my own writing, and vice versa. Since completing work on my first collection of stories, I have become more and more involved in translating contemporary Swiss fiction. Huge thanks to Vrony Jaeggi, Martin Zingg, and everyone behind the Solothurner Literaturtage; to the Literature team at Pro Helvetia; to colleagues at Translation House Looren; to those behind the translation workshops in Leuk, and the International Literature Festival in Leukerbad; and to writer friends such as Franco Supino, Pedro Lenz, Arno Camenisch, Urs Widmer, & Christoph Simon. I have not forgotten my background in German-German, and wish also to thank my colleagues at the Goethe Institute in Glasgow & London; the LCB in Berlin; and everyone involved in the German/English version of the *ViceVersa* workshops. Grateful thanks also to publishers with a firm commitment to literature in translation, such as Seagull Books, And Other Stories, & Dalkey Archive.

That books happen is great. Getting to present them to audiences, a bonus. For invitations to read at events, my thanks go this time round to the Scottish Writers' Centre in Glasgow, the Edinburgh International Book Festival, the Irish Writers' Centre, the Cork World Book Fest, the Dublin Writers' Festival, the Belfast Book

Festival, the Solothurner Literaturtage (again!), the Prose Days in Riga, and the European Literary Days in Lithuania. My thanks also to all those teachers in German, French, & Swiss schools who have organised readings for me in recent years. And to Paula Deitz of the *Hudson Review* for involving me, in Harlem and Newark, in her exciting "Writers in the Schools" programme.

I remain indebted to the now retired Derek Rodger of Argyll Publishing for running with my first collection.

Huge thanks, too, to the wonderful people at Dalkey Archive. To John O'Brien who asked to see my next book. To Jeremy Davies, with whom it is always a pleasure to work. To Jonathan Dykes for that great conversation on the train from Dublin to Cork. And to copy editor Sydney Weinberg for her sensitive response to my work.

I am grateful to Colum McCann, Kiran Desai and Peter Orner for their friendship and support. And remain touched by their response to my work.

Last but not least: my thanks—as ever—to the family & friends I would not be without.

donalmclaughlin.wordpress.com

MICHAL AJVAZ, *The Golden Age.*
The Other City.

PIERRE ALBERT-BIROT, *Grabinoulor.*

YUZ ALESHKOVSKY, *Kangaroo.*

FELIPE ALFAU, *Chromos.*
Locos.

IVAN ÂNGELO, *The Celebration.*
The Tower of Glass.

ANTÓNIO LOBO ANTUNES,
Knowledge of Hell.
The Splendor of Portugal.

ALAIN ARIAS-MISSON, *Theatre of Incest.*

JOHN ASHBERY & JAMES SCHUYLER,
A Nest of Ninnies.

ROBERT ASHLEY, *Perfect Lives.*

GABRIELA AVIGUR-ROTEM,
Heatwave and Crazy Birds.

DJUNA BARNES, *Ladies Almanack.*
Ryder.

JOHN BARTH, *Letters.*
Sabbatical.

DONALD BARTHELME, *The King.*
Paradise.

SVETISLAV BASARA, *Chinese Letter.*

MIQUEL BAUÇÀ, *The Siege in the Room.*

RENÉ BELLETTO, *Dying.*

MAREK BIENCZYK, *Transparency.*

ANDREI BITOV, *Pushkin House.*

ANDREJ BLATNIK, *You Do Understand.*

LOUIS PAUL BOON, *Chapel Road.*
My Little War.
Summer in Termuren.

ROGER BOYLAN, *Killoyle.*

IGNÁCIO DE LOYOLA BRANDÃO,
Anonymous Celebrity.
Zero.

BONNIE BREMSER, *Troia: Mexican
Memoirs.*

CHRISTINE BROOKE-ROSE,
Amalgamemnon.

BRIGID BROPHY, *In Transit.*

GERALD L. BRUNS,
Modern Poetry and the Idea of Language.

GABRIELLE BURTON, *Heartbreak Hotel.*

MICHEL BUTOR, *Degrees.*
Mobile.

G. CABRERA INFANTE,
Infante's Inferno.
Three Trapped Tigers.

JULIETA CAMPOS,
The Fear of Losing Eurydice.

ANNE CARSON, *Eros the Bittersweet.*

ORLY CASTEL-BLOOM, *Dolly City.*

LOUIS-FERDINAND CÉLINE,
Castle to Castle.
Conversations with Professor Y.
London Bridge.
Normance.
North.
Rigadoon.

MARIE CHAIX,
The Laurels of Lake Constance.

HUGO CHARTERIS, *The Tide Is Right.*

ERIC CHEVILLARD, *Demolishing Nisard.*

MARC CHOLODENKO, *Mordechai
Schamz.*

JOSHUA COHEN, *Witz.*

EMILY HOLMES COLEMAN,
The Shutter of Snow.

ROBERT COOVER, *A Night at the Movies.*

STANLEY CRAWFORD, *Log of the S.S.
The
Mrs Unguentine.*
Some Instructions to My Wife.

RENÉ CREVEL, *Putting My Foot in It.*

RALPH CUSACK, *Cadenza.*

NICHOLAS DELBANCO,
The Count of Concord.
Sherbrookes.

NIGEL DENNIS, *Cards of Identity.*

PETER DIMOCK,
A Short Rhetoric for Leaving the Family.

ARIEL DORFMAN, *Konfidenz.*

COLEMAN DOWELL, *Island People.*
Too Much Flesh and Jabez.

ARKADII DRAGOMOSHCHENKO,
Dust.

RIKKI DUCORNET,
The Complete Butcher's Tales.
The Fountains of Neptune.
The Jade Cabinet.
Phosphor in Dreamland.

WILLIAM EASTLAKE, *The Bamboo Bed.*
Castle Keep.
Lyric of the Circle Heart.

JEAN ECHENOZ, *Chopin's Move.*

STANLEY ELKIN, *A Bad Man.*
Criers and Kibitzers, Kibitzers and Criers.
The Dick Gibson Show.
The Franchiser.
The Living End.
Mrs. Ted Bliss.

FRANÇOIS EMMANUEL,
Invitation to a Voyage.

SALVADOR ESPRIU,
Ariadne in the Grotesque Labyrinth.

LESLIE A. FIEDLER,
Love and Death in the American Novel.

JUAN FILLOY, *Op Oloop.*

ANDY FITCH, *Pop Poetics.*

GUSTAVE FLAUBERT,
Bouvard and Pécuchet.

KASS FLEISHER, *Talking out of School.*

FORD MADOX FORD,
The March of Literature.

JON FOSSE, *Aliss at the Fire.*
Melancholy.

MAX FRISCH, *I'm Not Stiller.*
Man in the Holocene.

CARLOS FUENTES, *Christopher Unborn.*
Distant Relations.
Terra Nostra.
Where the Air Is Clear.

TAKEHIKO FUKUNAGA,
Flowers of Grass.

WILLIAM GADDIS, JR., *The Recognitions.*

JANICE GALLOWAY, *Foreign Parts.*
The Trick Is to Keep Breathing.

WILLIAM H. GASS,
Cartesian Sonata and Other Novellas.
Finding a Form.
A Temple of Texts.
The Tunnel.
Willie Masters' Lonesome Wife.

GÉRARD GAVARRY, *Hoppla! 1 2 3.*

ETIENNE GILSON,
The Arts of the Beautiful.Forms and Substances in the Arts.

C. S. GISCOMBE, *Giscome Road.*
Here.

DOUGLAS GLOVER,
Bad News of the Heart.

WITOLD GOMBROWICZ,
A Kind of Testament.

PAULO EMÍLIO SALES GOMES,
P's Three Women.

GEORGI GOSPODINOV, *Natural Novel.*

JUAN GOYTISOLO, *Count Julian.*
Juan the Landless.
Makbara.
Marks of Identity.

HENRY GREEN, *Back.*
Blindness.
Concluding.
Doting.
Nothing.

JACK GREEN, *Fire the Bastards!*

JIŘÍ GRUŠA, *The Questionnaire.*

MELA HARTWIG,
Am I a Redundant Human Being?

JOHN HAWKES, *The Passion Artist.*
Whistlejacket.

ELIZABETH HEIGHWAY, ED.,
Contemporary Georgian Fiction.

ALEKSANDAR HEMON, ED.,
Best European Fiction.

AIDAN HIGGINS, *Balcony of Europe.*
 Blind Man's Bluff
 Bornholm Night-Ferry.
 Flotsam and Jetsam.
 Langrishe, Go Down.
 Scenes from a Receding Past.

KEIZO HINO, *Isle of Dreams.*

KAZUSHI HOSAKA, *Plainsong.*

ALDOUS HUXLEY, *Antic Hay.*
 Crome Yellow.
 Point Counter Point.
 Those Barren Leaves.
 Time Must Have a Stop.

NAOYUKI II, *The Shadow of a Blue Cat.*

GERT JONKE, *The Distant Sound.*
 Geometric Regional Novel.
 Homage to Czerny.
 The System of Vienna.

JACQUES JOUET, *Mountain R.*
 Savage.
 Upstaged.

MIEKO KANAI, *The Word Book.*

YORAM KANIUK, *Life on Sandpaper.*

HUGH KENNER, *Flaubert.*
 Joyce and Beckett: The Stoic Comedians.
 Joyce's Voices.

DANILO KIŠ, *The Attic.*
 Garden, Ashes.
 The Lute and the Scars
 Psalm 44.
 A Tomb for Boris Davidovich.

ANITA KONKKA, *A Fool's Paradise.*

GEORGE KONRÁD, *The City Builder.*

TADEUSZ KONWICKI,
 A Minor Apocalypse.
 The Polish Complex.

MENIS KOUMANDAREAS, *Koula.*

ELAINE KRAF, *The Princess of 72nd Street.*

JIM KRUSOE, *Iceland.*

AYSE KULIN,
 Farewell: A Mansion in Occupied Istanbul.

EMILIO LASCANO TEGUI,
 On Elegance While Sleeping.

ERIC LAURRENT, *Do Not Touch.*

VIOLETTE LEDUC, *La Bâtarde.*

EDOUARD LEVÉ, *Autoportrait.*
 Suicide.

MARIO LEVI, *Istanbul Was a Fairy Tale.*

DEBORAH LEVY, *Billy and Girl.*

JOSÉ LEZAMA LIMA, *Paradiso.*

ROSA LIKSOM, *Dark Paradise.*

OSMAN LINS, *Avalovara.*
 The Queen of the Prisons of Greece.

ALF MAC LOCHLAINN,
 The Corpus in the Library.
 Out of Focus.

RON LOEWINSOHN, *Magnetic Field(s).*

MINA LOY, *Stories and Essays of Mina Loy.*

D. KEITH MANO, *Take Five.*

MICHELINE AHARONIAN MARCOM,
 The Mirror in the Well.

BEN MARCUS,
 The Age of Wire and String.

WALLACE MARKFIELD, *Teitlebaum's Window.*
 To an Early Grave.

DAVID MARKSON, *Reader's Block.*
 Wittgenstein's Mistress.

CAROLE MASO, *AVA.*

LADISLAV MATEJKA &
KRYSTYNA POMORSKA, EDS.,
 Readings in Russian Poetics: Formalist and Structuralist Views.

HARRY MATHEWS, *Cigarettes.*
 The Conversions.
 The Human Country: New and Collected Stories.
 The Journalist.
 My Life in CIA.
 Singular Pleasures.
 The Sinking of the Odradek.
 Stadium.
 Tlooth.

JOSEPH MCELROY,
 Night Soul and Other Stories.

ABDELWAHAB MEDDEB, *Talismano.*

GERHARD MEIER, *Isle of the Dead.*

HERMAN MELVILLE,
 The Confidence-Man.

AMANDA MICHALOPOULOU, *I'd Like.*

STEVEN MILLHAUSER,
 The Barnum Museum.
 In the Penny Arcade.

RALPH J. MILLS, JR., *Essays on Poetry.*

MOMUS, *The Book of Jokes.*

CHRISTINE MONTALBETTI,
 The Origin of Man.
 Western.

OLIVE MOORE, *Spleen.*

NICHOLAS MOSLEY, *Accident.*
 Assassins.
 Catastrophe Practice.
 Experience and Religion.
 A Garden of Trees.
 Hopeful Monsters.
 Imago Bird.
 Impossible Object.
 Inventing God.
 Judith.
 Look at the Dark.
 Natalie Natalia.
 Serpent.
 Time at War.

WARREN MOTTE,
 *Fables of the Novel: French Fiction
 since 1990.*
 Fiction Now:
 The French Novel in the 21st Century.
 Oulipo: A Primer of Potential Literature.

GERALD MURNANE, *Barley Patch.*
 Inland.

YVES NAVARRE, *Our Share of Time.*
 Sweet Tooth.

DOROTHY NELSON, *In Night's City.*
 Tar and Feathers.

ESHKOL NEVO, *Homesick.*

WILFRIDO D. NOLLEDO,
 But for the Lovers.

FLANN O'BRIEN, *At Swim-Two-Birds.*
 The Best of Myles.
 The Dalkey Archive.
 The Hard Life.
 The Poor Mouth.
 The Third Policeman.

CLAUDE OLLIER, *The Mise-en-Scène.*
 Wert and the Life Without End.

GIOVANNI ORELLI, *Walaschek's Dream.*

PATRIK OUŘEDNÍK, *Europeana.*
 The Opportune Moment, 1855.

BORIS PAHOR, *Necropolis.*

FERNANDO DEL PASO,
 News from the Empire.
 Palinuro of Mexico.

ROBERT PINGET, *The Inquisitory.*
 Mahu or The Material.
 Trio.

MANUEL PUIG, *Betrayed by Rita
 Hayworth.*
 The Buenos Aires Affair.
 Heartbreak Tango.

RAYMOND QUENEAU, T*he Last Days.*
 Odile.
 Pierrot Mon Ami.
 Saint Glinglin.

ANN QUIN, *Berg.*
 Passages.
 Three.
 Tripticks.

ISHMAEL REED, *The Free-Lance
 Pallbearers.*
 The Last Days of Louisiana Red.
 Ishmael Reed: The Plays.
 Juice!
 Reckless Eyeballing.
 The Terrible Threes.
 The Terrible Twos.
 Yellow Back Radio Broke-Down.

JASIA REICHARDT,
 15 Journeys Warsaw to London.

NOËLLE REVAZ, *With the Animals.*

JOÃO UBALDO RIBEIRO,
 House of the Fortunate Buddhas.

JEAN RICARDOU, *Place Names.*

RAINER MARIA RILKE,
The Notebooks of Malte Laurids Brigge.

JULIÁN RÍOS, The House of Ulysses.
Larva: A Midsummer Night's Babel.
Poundemonium.
Procession of Shadows.

AUGUSTO ROA BASTOS, *I the Supreme.*

DANIËL ROBBERECHTS,
Arriving in Avignon.

JEAN ROLIN,
The Explosion of the Radiator Hose.

OLIVIER ROLIN, *Hotel Crystal.*

ALIX CLEO ROUBAUD, *Alix's Journal.*

JACQUES ROUBAUD,
*The Form of a City Changes Faster, Alas,
Than
the Human Heart.*
The Great Fire of London.
Hortense in Exile.
Hortense Is Abducted.
The Loop.
*Mathematics: The Plurality of Worlds of
Lewis.*
The Princess Hoppy.
Some Thing Black.

RAYMOND ROUSSEL,
Impressions of Africa.

VEDRANA RUDAN, *Night.*

STIG SÆTERBAKKEN, *Siamese.*
Self Control.

LYDIE SALVAYRE, *The Company of Ghosts.*
The Lecture.
The Power of Flies.

LUIS RAFAEL SÁNCHEZ,
Macho Camacho's Beat.

SEVERO SARDUY, *Cobra & Maitreya.*

NATHALIE SARRAUTE,
Do You Hear Them?
Martereau.
The Planetarium.

ARNO SCHMIDT, *Collected Novellas.*
Collected Stories.
Nobodaddy's Children.
Two Novels.

ASAF SCHURR, *Motti.*

GAIL SCOTT, *My Paris.*

DAMION SEARLS,
*What We Were Doing and Where We Were
Going.*

JUNE AKERS SEESE,
Is This What Other Women Feel Too?
What Waiting Really Means.

BERNARD SHARE, *Inish.*
Transit.

VIKTOR SHKLOVSKY, *Bowstring.*
Knight's Move.
*A Sentimental Journey: Memoirs
1917–1922.*
Energy of Delusion: A Book on Plot.
Literature and Cinematography.
Theory of Prose.
Third Factory.
Zoo, or Letters Not about Love.

PIERRE SINIAC, *The Collaborators.*

KJERSTI A. SKOMSVOLD,
The Faster I Walk, the Smaller I Am.

JOSEF ŠKVORECKÝ,
The Engineer of Human Souls.

GILBERT SORRENTINO,
Aberration of Starlight.
Blue Pastoral.
Crystal Vision.
Imaginative Qualities of Actual Things.
Mulligan Stew.
Pack of Lies.
Red the Fiend.
The Sky Changes.
Something Said.
Splendide-Hôtel.
Steelwork.
Under the Shadow.

W. M. SPACKMAN, *The Complete Fiction.*

ANDRZEJ STASIUK, *Dukla.*
Fado.